I0579539

LOVE

&

DARTS

Stories

By

NATH JONES

LIFE LIST PRESS
CHICAGO · 2015

Life List Press
Chicago, IL

PREVIOUSLY PUBLISHED

Jones, Nath. "Limbic Resonance: Responses to a Match.com Questionnaire." *The Battered Suitcase* 3.4 (2011): 40-41. *Issuu*. Vagabondage Press, 1 Mar. 2011. Web. 29 Dec. 2011. <http://issuu.com/vagabondagepress/docs/tbs10301>.

Jones, Nath. "Should: How Mommy Ate Her Soul." *PANK Magazine* March (2010). *PANK Magazine*. PANK, 3 May 2010. Web. 29 Dec. 2011. <http://www.pankmagazine.com/nath-jones/>.

Jones, Nath. "Tandem." *From the Edge of the Prairie* 8 (2011): 6-13. Print.

PUBLISHER'S NOTE

These selections are works of fiction. Names, characters, places, and incidents are either the product of the author's imagination or are used fictionally and any resemblance to actual persons, living or dead, business establishments, events, or locales is entirely coincidental

ISBN-10: 1937316149
ISBN-13: 978-1-937316-14-3

Book design by Gin Y. Havard
Author photo by Louisa Podlich
Cover image by Yulia Drozdova

Printed in the United States of America

For Amy & Bill,

most merciful friends

Karen's Krew

Karen's Krew at F.O.E. #2548 -- L to R: Jim ROOSTER Wisely, JOELBACON Haskell, Karen SPECIAL K McAleer, BIG JOE Gembala, & Kayla KATE Reyes.

ACKNOWLEDGMENTS

Lucille Fridley * Gin Havard * Rebecca Montalvo * Jane Friedman * Leah Jones * Anita Jordan * Vanessa Shivla * John Philip McGraw * Andrew Zimmerman Jones * Nate Dean * Dariusz Janecki * Chris Howard * Becky Holzman * Erin Gunderson * Tammy Servies * Pepper Burkholder * Xavier Rodriguez * Melanie Callahan Willhite (aka Mrs. Awesomeness) * Mike Moreth * Chris McGovern * Beth Prusiecki * Tom Arnold * Tom Martin * Michele Bultman Tracy * Larisa Parrish * Andres Jimenez * Alan Larson * Jennifer Wohlberg * Maria Kubiak * Erin Boudreaux * Elizabeth Munroz * Josh Sipes * Reginald Gibbons * Sandi Wisenberg * Patrick Somerville * the creative writing faculty at Northwestern University * The Batasses * The Bowlemics * my Facebook family * Pat Bruce * Robert Sowder * Darren Mast * Rick Hall (and Sally, Crystal, & Sherrie) * Roger & Judy Beehler * Lila & Jakie Houts * Andrew Groh * Dorothy Jones

The quality of mercy is not strained,

It droppeth as the gentle rain from heaven

Upon the place beneath. It is twice blest:

It blesseth him that gives and him that takes.

—William Shakespeare, *The Merchant of Venice*

CONTENTS

UNTIL THEY SHINE

They denied sharing sweet laughter. Romance wasn't the point. After one thirty in the morning, she took him inside, down a shotgun hallway, into the living room, and left him there. In a way he was an enemy loved. This oil rig welder who'd been all over the world stood half turning back to see where she'd gone and half looking around to see where he was in this needs-some-more-wall-art silence. It was the beginning of the one hour before he found his way into her smile.

She did not know him, though.

There are those long-faithful loves properly absent in the world, old minefield loves, where two safe souls waltz around each other in the well-patrolled confines of a security setting—picking conversations to have about logistics, relying on favorites, looking at comfort food photos on 4x6 cards, giving annual gifts meaning nothing to the rest of the world. But there are also extreme momentary loves, ready to be smashed and forgotten, or, more often, intimately eaten alive.

She didn't really invite him. And he didn't exactly say he'd come. But there he was at her place without the music that probably should have been playing. Not long. The girl he found under a night-lit skylight came back with ginger vodka drinks, an unnecessary seduction. And so these two were socially imperative like that for an hour before the start-gate release of their mutual moving on. One of them giggled. The other, respectfully, pretended it hadn't just happened. She straddled him, leaned forward, kissed him, kissed his neck. He lifted her up, turned her around, pulled her back down onto his lap and pressed his hand into everything he didn't think was exactly perfect.

An hour and forty-five minutes ago the bartender's finger hovered over the button that controlled the totalizer system. She'd accidentally—well, so what if it were staged?—elbowed the oil rig man in the ribs. But hard enough to force a conversation at an Irish pub when she got bored with the practiced words of student lawyers. God. She tired of those lofty boys' aspirations, their talk of how it all should be—how it would all have to be—and so she turned on their convictions, gravitated toward this other man in jeans and an undisclosed smile.

This guy wasn't so sure of how things should be—would all have to be—or at least he didn't say. He just reached one hand out to her hip, put his fingers down into her waistband, bent his arm so she stepped forward between his knees while he put his other hand around her back, pulled her in even closer and said, "Hi." She said, "Not really." So he didn't ask any more questions. He'd been practicing his story and told her he tied oil rigs to the ocean floor with heat enough to weld what's desired to what's real. She didn't understand. It was his job to dive over oil under the sea and join steel to steel two hundred feet down in the black.

He made promises easily like a man who never took physics in high school. But not to her. There was no point. She didn't want or expect any of that. So he didn't bother. He just laughed for the girl he found in the bar, broad telling of his eight weeks with the winter ocean's twenty-five-foot swells, how those furious, feminine seas could very likely scour him off with their daily washing. "You get pretty knocked around. Gotta be tethered or you're gone."

She pretended not to notice or care.

He showed her, demonstrated the harness that held him and mimed the length that tied him to the rig. He told her about being sealed skin to soul by that North

Sea's frigid wanting. A man of faith—two hundred feet down in the black. Just a man, a steel-making man, on the water all winter, robbing the layered sea floor. So what? Why should she be impressed? That woman—young woman—was not the North Sea, not the water, not anything to tether himself to. She was the way he used to be: quiet, nostalgic, and true. But now he's less easily baited. He's heavenly-ride-the-rode-down-bluebell and Honduras blends whiskey, too.

New Orleans, a port city, still rocks and sways with him as he shows her the ashes of the Irish owner behind the bar, asks about her travels, her school, her under-the-water-pressured lubrication, asks—with final kindness—if she'd like a beer. Laughing hard, with his hands on this small out-of-town girl (refusing to be scoured off) she says yes. It is the only answer. Two hundred feet of foregone conclusion wrap him desultorily without words and yet, she drifts free—when anyone knows oil is best suited for floating. Like you, she's been told that babies will wake her in the morning part of the night. Funny how people will pay to let you borrow their children for a while. But there is nothing to babysit underneath the sea. That man lives in relief, opposite, pressured from all sides by our foundations: oil, steel, the ocean floor. So she knows in the morning she will wake up and ask him to leave.

Sometimes—never when she waits—her mind reels hapless in possibility.

But this time she will not let it.

Even under the North Sea's mighty pressured weight, he'll disrespect her repression, override her compression. He'll steel-make and can rise up—with a flame down deep—drilling oil for freighters to drink. So neither of the two of them takes bars and beer for granted. They say nothing and let their eyes work. In her mind she explores his deep sea diving welds and lets him come up through it all covered in oil. And for him she goes down into everything, into the sea changed, thinking of him there, two hundred feet down in the black.

"We can walk to my place from here." She will never admit to being a power-monger, a tyrant, but his telling her no is unacceptable.

They're at her front door again—right before she held his hand and led him down that shotgun hallway to begin their awkward-fondling preliminary hour of what would be their fifteen-minute forever. And they both see it on the porch: everything that will happen in an hour. There's no power of attorney. A simple consent is all that's necessary for his body, riding an eddy current and sloshing over some forgotten bank, to be never so golden-gilt or at all, so easy does the wick go free.

They're inside the apartment. Her eyes flick quickly, realizing what a mess she's about to bring him into but he sees nothing. She knows everything that's not good enough. Not him. Not the door. Not the scented amber candle on the speaker, the one she's about to ask if he'd like for her to light. Not the belts and bras hanging from their hooks in her bathroom that she should have put away. Not the dracaena growing tall in the window. Not the catcher's mitt on the floor. Not the rumpled clothes burying a red rocking chair. Not the TV stand where the pepper grinder's left forgotten. Not the unopened stack of mail shifting, losing its balance on the desk. Not the beach hats rarely worn or her grandmother's heirloom painting where a tugboat forever pulls a man on a barge over silk-rippling waters. Her eyes flick on, wishful-cleaning as they go.

They have to get through this hour to get to the well of not wanting more. Neither of them is dutiful. They just wait it out. Hoping one will go for the other as soon as possible. His gaze is upon her and then—because she seems so nervous—he takes it off her again and plants both eyes upon the man in the painting who is standing on the barge with his back to the painter. He doesn't admit a knowledge of art but wonders what it is to feel a ruddy perennially burning sun through that sweaty, dingy oil-canvas tee shirt and half-dry pair of pants. What kind of forever would it be to stand on the stillness of a moving barge that's being towed by a tugboat through a painting? Why paint a person backwards like that with one arm up, untired, waving to someone else hidden in the trees on the far side of the river? He doesn't care and his eyes are upon her again.

Somehow the hour passes. Twenty minutes in, she takes the vodka and ginger glasses to the sink and finds three cans of beer in her crisper. She shouts a question from the kitchen. He says not to worry about it. He's got a condom.

Forty minutes in she's less nervous and notices him looking at the painting again, says, "Do you think he's leaving or just arrived? Waving like that?"

Fifty minutes in, he smiles to her and, again, for the last time, it's already happened right there before everything. With nine minutes left he puts his hand on her thigh. At five he takes her to the floor. He is a river between them with that eddying-dentist's-drill way of going on carving away the soft easy places to rush through. And finally he falls on her, kissing on and on without malice.

She didn't ever ask what music he likes. Didn't figure she'd want to listen to it for that hour, sitting together, quiet on a blue corduroy couch with two threadbare cushions and a pristine third. She didn't even bother to turn on the TV.

For those dredged minutes of putting off passion, she stared at all her electronics and was igneous. Stillness left of heat and motion. Her silent mouth echoed with gunshots and doom in that cavity fortified by a perimeter of teeth. But they didn't need to talk. If some hinged midnight swung open and crashed complex over the minds of any willing listeners begotten of forgotten mothers, could there have been a resurrection? No. The hour goes by and the clothes get lost with everything else that's not good enough. They're finally sweating naked without having to get through undoing anything. His nature, with one foot on the floor, two hands against the wall and his common ground inside her own, seems all the more damned. As if fright and courage were not twins, as if breath were not divided by passion held, and as if bright harnessed lives did night sing.

But yes, worth everything, his shoulders rub her harder-to-reach, harder-to-understand solid ways of loving until they shine, polished wet and recede, giving out and arriving, filling some flood plain, some untouched me-part of both-them, some world so often dry, now saturated and ready for continual living. Under that patient fury; his

waterway; his easy-to-abandon God.

DRIVE

At eleven o'clock that morning she asked me to take her for a drive.

I held her too tightly walking out of the restaurant and back to the car, I remember that. So I guess I sort of knew. But not really. Not like she did.

She knew.

I know she knew.

My Grandma Charlottie was sweet, skinny, sinewy, white, sleeves-rolled-up, slow-walking, tobacco-spit-sprayed pants—I don't even know how that happened—and a kind of full-upper-body head-turn that's hard to believe. God damn. She was tiny. But sometimes she'd look at you like she was about to haul off and whack you with a remote control before she'd smile and walk away like nothing ever happened.

I'd been thinking about whether or not to refurbish the utility room. I don't know who did the sheet metal work in there but the seams are opening up. No matter how high we set the thermostat that furnace can't warm up any room for all the heat that escapes.

When she asked to go for that drive she hadn't been in a car in eight months. My dumb ass took it as a sign of improvement. I said, "Sure. Where you wanna go, Grandma?"

I used to pick up the prescriptions after her radiation treatments. I remember waiting for something called Magic Mouthwash. The girl in the pharmacy said it would take a little longer because they have to mix it up special. I said, "What's in it?" The girl—she wasn't really pretty or anything—said, "Something to coat the ulcerations. Something else to numb the whole area. She can use it every few hours. Whenever she feels her throat burn." I said, "Fine. I'll wait."

And I did. I was patient. Read an issue of *Car & Driver*. I remember that's when I called my friend back about the job in his garage—not that I want to put tires on cars my whole life. But. It's good money for a while and he didn't do a credit check. Anyway.

She hadn't been in a car in eight months and then she said, "Take me up 421. Would you, please?"

Polite and poor. That's what the minister should have said in her eulogy. Not that twenty-minute story about her going to Duluth for a typing job for two months. Who gives a shit about Duluth? That wasn't her. That's only two months. The rest of the time she was here, with us.

But I'm glad we went for that drive.

Her shirt was covered with her own blood spat out and dried up. But there was no other shirt. Mom put 'em all away when we thought hospice was a place she had to go. So I didn't say she should change. Grandma's bare arm was thin and the skin gathered at her elbow and again at her wrist. Weird skin. Kind of yellow. Almost like you could see through it. I wasn't thinking when I grabbed for her sweater. I forgot it only had one sleeve because my sister cut the other one off to start making an afghan. Well. It would have been a nice afghan if she didn't give up trying to do a whole blanket to help keep Grandma warm, if there was more time, more yarn.

Grandma Charlottie pretended not to notice the cockroaches running in all directions when I picked up her sweater.

I pretended not to notice, too. Just shook it real good.

And I guess I was sort of pissed about there only being one sleeve when I helped her put it on. I was mainly pissed at myself for forgetting. But then I was pissed at my sister for even trying to make an afghan out of her favorite sweater. Grandma just went ahead and let me put that one-armed sweater on her, you know, went through the motions, seemed not to notice what was undone and missing.

We had the heat on because she was always cold. Even that morning. Even though it was summer. Damn ducts in the bedroom need to be repaired, too. I shifted my weight back and forth while I helped her with the sweater. I could feel a stream of hot air coming through a crack in the metal. I'd move my body into it so I could feel it on my head and then move it back to get away.

I could just kick myself for putting that sweater on her. I didn't think about dignity. I just wanted her to stay a little bit warm and I didn't know it was the last time I'd ever get to take her anywhere. I would have gone upstairs and gotten one of Mom's blouses maybe or at least had her put on Dad's old hunting jacket. It's so stupid. I was trying to put the sweater on her to cover up the mess on her shirt and the sweater just made everything a hundred times worse.

Ten years ago she would've tore my head off for putting her in a sweater like that. She must've been pretty far gone already that morning.

I knew about my sister's project the instant Grandma's tiny, veiny arm came through where that sleeve was supposed to be. But I didn't remember when I saw the sweater on the floor by her bed. When I grabbed it up and shook it and started to help her into it, it was still just Grandma's favorite sweater in my mind. She wore that thing every day of the winter for years. It's weird how that happens. Isn't it? I mean you know something's changed but because it was always the same forever you only remember it a certain way.

I don't know if she cared or not. She let me help her with the sweater and the door and the steps and the seat belt.

When she said she wanted to head up 421 I thought maybe she wanted to go to the cemetery to see Grandpa. But she didn't ask and we passed all those quiet plots under trees without mention. The sun flashed off gravestones as we went by. The shadows and sun bred some kind of almost-like-hope on the grass.

You know what I'm talking about. I'm talking about driving fast on a sunny day with a bunch of birds—barn swallows probably—on the telephone wires. And when the rush of wind, that updraft from your car coming, hits them they rise and scatter and you can't watch them all flying off in all directions like that. You can just look at the grass in the ditch and see their fluttering shadows dispersing. Then maybe your eye does follow the one that flies straight out in front of you, like it can maybe almost stay ahead of you, maybe fly right alongside the car for a second, or at least keep up if it flaps hard enough. But then you're gone and the bird behind you that was out in front banks right over the fields and disappears.

I remember everything.

Early summer. The earth seemed so willing. But after so much negotiation what would not?

The horizon seemed to give in to the call for more flat corn and patches of distant trees. A farmhouse, wearing out its paint job, with bikes for sale near the road, all in a row, biggest to smallest, had its screen door standing wide open. Probably got stuck in the porch roof. I always wonder why there are so many bikes in front of one house. I wondered that then. Like usual.

It was all how it always is on that drive. We passed the fairgrounds. Quiet before a raucous week in July. We passed the county airport and the county jail. The place where the city keeps the snowplows, the towering cone of street salt. The cow corn was knee-high. Green against that wet black between rows.

And we passed the radio station broadcasting the price of pork bellies and soybean futures up and out into the unreceptive sky.

Nearing the interstate the businesses sprang up again. McDonald's. Amoco. BP. A fireworks barn. Some kind of truck stop where they sell laser-engraved blocks of crystal that eagles fly through for whatever reason.

I remember I said, "You want something, Grandma?" 'Cause I didn't know if she wanted to just drive or maybe if she wanted to stop.

I probably shouldn't have looked over at her right then, you know? I probably should have just let her have her moment. But I didn't know. I'd been driving. I didn't mean to look over at her. It just happened. When I saw that she was crying it almost made me cry.

You know how it is. With everyone else it's no big deal. When I drive my girlfriend around I look at the road and then I look over at her to ask her stuff. Same with Mom. Or Dad when I drop him off at work sometimes. You know. I just ask them stuff. What music they want to listen to. Whether they want the air conditioner on. If they need me to get them anything from the Dollar Store later, since it's right by the garage where I work. And my girlfriend, my mom, my dad, they're never crying real quiet like that in the passenger seat, you know? That never happens. That's what makes me think she knew. And her knowing makes me feel like I should have known and not ever put that sweater on her. But how could I have known?

I'd give anything not to have looked over at her when I asked if she wanted anything. I hate what I saw. But once it was done what could I do? I just handed her an Arby's napkin.

She gripped that thing, stopped crying real quick—like it never happened—straightened up, and said, "Bob Evans."

I rolled the window down on my side for the rest of the drive. I wasn't really choking back tears, you know. I just needed the air to keep more alert. Can't hardly breathe all cooped up inside a car.

I said, "Grandma Charlottie?"

She said, "Yes."

"I'm not sure I can do the repairs myself. It's a big job."

She didn't respond. I don't know if it was because she was disappointed in me or because she knew there was no money to hire a heating and cooling guy or if she just didn't really care anymore. Because I think she knew, you know?

When we got to the restaurant I helped her with the seat belt, the curb, the steps, and the hostess. We sat at the counter. It was easier to lean onto the stools than for her sit down in one of those low wooden chairs at the tables. The coffeepots sang silent with their steam. There was no one there who cared about her sweater. And we each ate biscuits. Turning so slow, swiveling from side-to-side on our almost-too-resistant counter stools.

CHARACTER SKETCH, 1997

She had to have it, you know? That was kind of her thing, real grabby-like.

But she was good at things that didn't rely on others. She was good at things for a little while and then moved on. She was good at things like mixing drinks and cooking; like making jewelry; arranging patio furniture under the setting Texan sun; gardening, tomatoes mainly; and playing video games. It's not like she was neat or whatever. But she liked things a certain way in a certain place and organized her CDs, rearranged the inside furniture, too. Alphabetized books on shelves. Stuff like that, you know. What else? Oh. She was really good at picking songs and burning homemade compilations for friends. Crafts, too. She made envelopes, you know.

Herself. By hand. Same with cigarettes and decoupage collages.

Yeah. I can tell you more. There's always more.

Mixing drinks: In a glass vase on the counter behind the sink she kept long glass swizzle sticks with bright ornamental figures on the tops. Blown glass, you know? A monkey. A parrot. A palm tree. And a bright umbrella. They were a set. An expensive set of art glass swizzle sticks. Kitschy but beautifully rendered. She was careful with them and for fun screamed at her friends to be careful with them too. It was like a joke, but super mean. She made the drinks in the kitchen. Stirred them with the handle end of a knife, then served them on the patio wearing their swizzle sticks, expecting comment. Tom Collins. Mint Julep. Gimlet. Clamato and Spicy Tequila with Lime Juice.

Cooking: She always used the right implement or pot for its express purpose. And she didn't mind the cleanup that this involved. She didn't mind at all. I know because she always told me, "I don't mind."

Making jewelry: She had a red Sears Craftsman toolbox where she kept all her jewelry-making supplies. The burliness was explained away. It was a really satisfying toolbox. In the top she kept all the beads in a carefully-organized removable tray. Underneath there were different wires and clasps and pairs of needle-nose pliers and graduated sizes of similar-looking tools. In the bottom of her butch jewelry-making box she also kept a paring knife. It had belonged to her great-grandfather who had come to America from Sweden via Ellis Island. She said he carved his initials in a lot of walls with that knife. She told the story saying she didn't approve of graffiti.

Gardening: Her garden was a tribute to her favorite architects. Bamboo structures were everywhere. She grew tomatoes on all of them except for the ones where peppers and sweet sugar snap peas with their "Awwww-look-aren't-they-sweet?" blossoms grew. But like Monet with his haystacks she had a focus and was mainly interested in the best structure to support tomatoes. Tried different things. Pyramids. Towers. Conical funnels. And round cages. She built whimsical bent-bamboo tomato trellis forts. After trying everything she found that an igloo-type structure provided the best support and ease of harvest for the tomatoes. It optimized the exposed surface area of the leaves to bright midday sunlight.

Video games: She was very good at video games that involved racing. She could even race the game itself on the most difficult and trying courses. She was, however, not so good at the video games that involved the martial arts. Her roundhouse kick was a personal embarrassment.

Organizing CDs: If a friend were depressed and there seemed no way to contribute, she would show up on a breezy Saturday and organize the CDs as if of course that would help. She put them in genres—not in alphabetical order like the books. And once finished she put the DVDs and videotapes away. And she would look under the sink and put order there. Then she would make sure that the clothes in closets were not chaotic but pleasantly satisfying, orderly. She'd make a joke from a movie about wire hangers. After that, she would link her arm in her friend's arm and they would find a place to eat tamales and chicken wings outside in the afternoon. "You'll love it. Their cheladas are great."

Arranging the furniture: The furniture in her living room was always a little discordant. She liked to have the bright yellow chaise next to her black metal apothecary chest right in front of the door as one walked in. It had an interesting effect. Not exactly feng shui. Coming into the room one was accosted by the fortress of furniture. But she had it that way for a reason. The person lying on the chaise could reach over and open the door without getting up. If the cops came, well, it bought time.

Burning songs: She was a fanatic with the CD burner. But she made it a moral point to buy exactly one quarter of the downloaded artists' songs.

Making envelopes: The artisan envelope was her signature. When she sent invitations for her cocktail parties, which she had on the patio with citronella torchlight, low funky music, and those fancy blown-glass swizzle sticks that she yelled at her friends to use with care, she made the invitation envelopes herself out of old wrapping paper or wallpaper samples. But the effort was so great that the guest lists stayed short.

Rolling cigarettes: She was very good at rolling cigarettes. She could do it in her hands. Or she could do it on her little cigarette-rolling machine that she took with her to diners late at night. Mostly it was tobacco.

Collages and decoupage: She collected pieces of wood. Mainly small, really quite useless cutting boards. She never used wooden cutting boards in her kitchen. Didn't like bacteria to breed at an uncontrollable rate. But they were such beautiful pieces of wood, those little cutting boards.

So she bought them, the smallest ones, the most useless ones, whenever she got the chance. She cut pictures of thin-armed girls in well-suited homes from magazines. *Dwell. Better Homes & Gardens. National Geographic.* And *Surf Digest.* She made collages on the cutting boards with decoupage glue and a pair of really sharp haircutting scissors from the beauty supply shop.

Planting terrariums in perfume bottles: Though short-lived, for a time she made a hobby of planting terrariums in tiny perfume bottles. She made a great terrarium and gave it to her elderly neighbor whose children had decided to sell the old woman's house and move her into an assisted living community. Who could blame them for the market? Houses just wouldn't ever get these kinds of prices again. But still. It didn't seem right to sell an old lady's house out from under her without her consent. So my friend with the jewelry-making toolbox and the art glass swizzle sticks and the optimal bamboo structure for growing tomatoes stayed up all night and planted a teeny tiny terrarium for her neighbor to take with her to her last new life.

Humming: But. You know how things go. There are ups and downs. Not everything is the way you might hope. My friend was just like anyone that way. She panicked. She threw things. She shoved people. She held close friends in vicious contempt. She was paranoid. She didn't care. She was defensive. She was wounded. She was on drugs but not like they teach you in school. She was above all that and did drugs for fun, for freedom, for something to do with her disposable income, for the hell of it, for the experience, for enough quality bonding time, for better sex, for enlightened transcendence and Whip-it! laughs. Sometimes she cried and screamed with an infantile sense of injustice. But. Whenever she was driving alone she was happy. And she hummed.

SMILES

Sometimes you are standing in line at the bank. And you smile because you feel you must. You don't expect to chat and converse but the teller is an old enemy from high school. You already know her story. You've heard five different versions of it. Worse. She knows yours.

You're in hot-pink sweatpants from Victoria's Secret. They're pulled up to mid-calf. And you don't remember in the moment that they were buy-one-get-a-free-purse-sized-perfume. You're wearing flip-flops with a row of rhinestones passing over the tan you rubbed on your feet, your belly, your shoulders, your legs. Your mother, every mother you know, used to say, "You can be anything, honey." She used to say, "We don't quit." Now she says, "I don't think you heard me the first time. I don't care who he is."

Your hair is a mess. And who gives a shit? It's ninety degrees and humid. You really weren't planning on seeing anyone anyway. Definitely not this chick.

Dammit. There's no avoiding her. She's already seen you and the other lady must be at lunch. You're next. You're waiting for your turn to reach out and grab a sucker from the baseball-shaped ceramic mug. You're behind the overweight guy in Wranglers, a dusty blue flannel work shirt, and big, red, wide suspenders. So what if she's looking at you, trying to wave a little bit, craning her neck around Mr. Can't-Wear-A-Belt-Like-A-Normal-Person to say hi before he's finished his business? Just stare all you want at the one brass clip on his waistband, which is slowly letting go of that denim edge. Metal fatigue, probably. The thing's got no grip left. It's gonna pop at any moment.

Your mother used to say, "Quit staring." But why should you? That thing is barely holding on and you want to see it spring loose the next time he heaves with one of those COPD coughs. What's the point of looking away? What's the deal with all this shame, all this pretending nothing's happening, all this putting a good face on a whole bunch of bullshit? And why should you do it for this guy in suspenders or for the old enemy from high school who counts a stack of twenties and keeps starting over? It's not pride or social etiquette. It is not prayer— that's elsewhere. There is no reason to pray for this girl or some old, fat guy with red suspenders. So just keep looking at that brass clip, which will definitely pop before he gets back to his truck, and let your mind start its usual subservient free fall.

You see that real unnamed breath, which never has explained itself. As if you care. You violently toss away your Bible school-issue halo but it boomerangs, chokes you, and spins around your neck like a fast, accurate horseshoe on a stake cemented against the force of arthritic clapping and victorious shouts by some great-uncle at a family reunion. And with this kind of physical proximity to the essence of life you know instantly and then know nothing of it, remembering the bank teller, this old enemy from high school, is divorced with two kids.

You should have just deposited this thing at the ATM but you can't now. You want a pineapple sucker and need a roll of quarters anyway. You shift your weight to place your body under the air conditioning vent. The man in the suspenders is finished with his business. He pounds a stack of envelopes on the counter and explains himself as he heads for the door, the truck, and the post office, which is under review. "Wouldn't have even had either overdraft fee if the payroll service didn't take the day off for the Fourth. Damn thing's automated. How's a computer gonna take the day off?" And he's gone.

The door is made of glass tinted brown.

Before you take that last step forward there is another glimmer in your mind but it is nothing fearful, nothing really intimidating, nothing that can hurt you. Not anymore. Those glimmers are good. They breed humility in your worldview, deference in decision-making, caution while driving, and hesitation in what you say. They are visitors that beguile certainty on tired afternoons, trespassers and traitors, like old friends lost, like space invaders.

But whatever. You don't have to look over your shoulder anymore. Just put your paycheck between your teeth, pull the boomerang/horseshoe/halo thing away from your throat, and readjust your headband. You don't have a duty to listen to this girl's sob story while she cashes your check.

You don't have to care. You don't. But you do need a roll of quarters. So you take that last step forward and smile. Just hand her the stupid paycheck and say it. "Hey. Girl. How've you been doing?"

You pick up the baseball-shaped coffee mug and start rifling through it looking for what you want.

She takes it as her cue to say she's recovering slowly from a bout of too much drinking which came out in the custody hearing—it's not as if she drives into oncoming traffic every day—but luckily they found in her favor. You do not care. But you still smile. So she goes on. She couldn't believe that the judge let him get out of paying the child support he'd missed: the child will only eat brand-name chicken nuggets, which are not cheap even if you buy in bulk. She moved back in with her mom and dad and they are helping her get back on her feet. She had to sell the house but that was okay because the roof needed to be replaced and the people that bought it knew some great roofers. She couldn't have afforded to put a roof on that house after all the court costs and divorce and all. But she's doing really well.

It's over. You've got the quarters. You've listened to whatever she felt the need to share. You're done. You turn to leave. You take a step away from the counter and have your sunglasses back on before she says, "And what about you? Did you decide to press charges?"

BLEACH & WHITE TOWELS

♡

After work—fuck that bullshit job—I get home and give in.

Sometimes I can't get back up off the couch all night. It's not any one thing. I just don't know what duties matter, what obligations I care about, or how much to let myself be exploited by these assholes who think one person can do six peoples' jobs. American dream. Are you freaking kidding me? Who the hell makes it happen? I don't see how it's possible. A house? Marriage? Kids?

I'm tapping the base of the entertainment center with my shoe and slouch down. My neck's bent against the back of the couch and my butt's hanging off the cushions. I'm glad I don't have a girlfriend. Dating's too expensive. One dinner and a movie and I can hardly pay my rent.

There's not crap on TV anymore. I throw a frozen French bread pizza in the toaster oven, go back to the couch, grab the remote, flip around for a while, watch some news, maybe a little SportsCenter, but what's the point?

The Brewers suck right now. They'll never amount to anything with Davey Lopes.

The timer reminds me to get up. By no stretch of the imagination is this pathetic pizza a supreme. There is one shaving of sausage and a layer of cheese I can see through on top of the thin slab of bread. Flakes of red and green pepper placed at statistically optimal distances from one another seem to repel the tiny cubes of pepperoni that dot the top.

Still. They don't cut corners on packaging. Some dude stares up at me from the pizza box in the trash. He's supposed to be a fighter pilot, an ideal. His red scarf is blowing back in the wind. His eyes are cast to the heavens beyond. Dashing. Dude's got a fucking mustache and a tousled animated haircut. He's wearing goggles on his head. And his stylized WWII garb would still get more women than I ever could.

I look at the clock. It's almost eight. Whether or not I show up, Judson's always got a shot of Tullamore Dew sitting in a glass on the bar for me at eight o'clock.

To have a drink waiting for you at the bar when you get there is a great sign of significance.

I don't really care that much.

But I usually go. Some people put on a new shirt to go out at night. I never do. I've never really understood it. I just go in my work clothes. The bar on the corner is brick, has a cracked set of curved cement steps that no one's ever gonna fix, and has too many neon signs for the size of the windows. There are two small Harleys parked on the sidewalk. Who the hell parks on the sidewalk?

I open the door and camel bells slap the back side. A few other regular patrons look up from listening to the bartender read out loud. He does that sometimes. Seems to get a kick out of it on slow nights. He holds a book and says, "And I am dirty with its satisfaction." I rattle the door, like applause maybe, like I'm sort of making fun of him, too. Nothing crazy. Nothing out of control. Just enough to bring him down a peg. The camel bells smack the wall once and Judson shuts the book. He doesn't look pissed and sure enough, my drink's waiting in front of my seat at the short end of the bar.

He looks me in the eye, "'And I am dirty with its satisfaction.' Isn't that great? So much in it. All the guilt. All the pleasure. All the social constructs and guises and norms and repression. I love it."

I drink slowly. "I'll love it when you get off the literary kick."

"Just waiting for Monday Night Football so the library card can go back in the closet. I can't stand baseball. Won't have it in this bar."

The Brewers suck anyway. "You got anything to eat back there?"

He starts to dig through a little fridge and produces half an egg salad sandwich, three jalapeno-pickled green beans that go in the Bloody Marys, and a fistful of pretzels stale from the humidity. He plops everything onto a paper plate that bends with the weight and shoves it over to me. "A little gold, frankincense, and myrrh for you, right there. How's that?"

Better than that crappy pizza. "I'm dirty with its satisfaction."

He turns his back, picks up a bucket, and heads for the ice maker. I watch him digging down into the chest of fused ice cubes. What the fuck is he using? Some kind of red plastic thing. "Is that a sand shovel for kids at the beach?"

"Yeah. It is."

I don't want to ask. But. I can't let it go. "Why the fuck are you using a sand shovel?"

"I don't know. I bought it last week. Thought it'd work pretty good. I hate those stainless steel scoops. The handles get too cold. And I don't like cutting ketchup jugs to make scoops either. Too much trouble. They bend and crack. This is sturdy."

"But it's a kid's toy."

"So."

There are two women playing pool. They don't talk too much but enjoy the game. One wears black leather pants. The other's in a black leather vest. They must account for the two Harleys outside. Nebraska plates. Nice bikes. But I don't know too much about bikes. I look at the woman in the vest a little too long. She smiles. She cocks her hips. She leans on the pool cue. She opens her mouth and touches her tongue to the tapering length of the wood.

Jesus. Who wants to deal with all that? I've gotta work in the morning. I swivel on my stool, put both elbows on the bar, and watch Judson dump ice over the beers. "Those girls in for Summerfest, you think? I'm not going this year. Too many people. Too much traffic."

"It's Harley's 100th though, too. That could be it. Or just traveling."

"The 100th was last year."

"Right." I can't eat egg salad sandwiches. Shit's nasty. "How's their game?"

"Better than yours. What do you think about my egg salad? Never made it before, but I had a craving."

"Not bad. Needs to be on toast though."

"Toast? I've never had egg salad on toast. I'll try it."

He gets summoned to the other end of the bar. I pick up a paper and suck on a green bean. I flip slowly through the Journal Sentinel. After a while Judson wanders back and starts washing glasses.

I hold up the paper, turn an article toward him so he can see the headline and photo. "Did you see this about Kenny Chesney and Uncle Kracker on Saturday? Bizarre."

"Yeah, the lineup's fucked this year. I used to know more of the smaller bands. Now I barely care."

We're silent for a little while. It gets later. More people start coming in. They fill up the bar around me and the bartender gets busy. I read an article about zoning regulations. I read another article about various parking tribulations for Summerfest. I read part two in a three-part series about the zebra mussel infestation in the Great Lakes and its damaging effects on the ecosystem. I say to Judson, "Have you ever heard of an invasive species?" But he doesn't answer. I keep reading. The mussels come from the Caspian Sea and other foreign ballast waters of oceangoing ships that come to port in Chicago, Detroit, and Green Bay. They make a hell of a mess of pipes apparently. I drink the High Life. The wet bottle makes rings on the newspaper. The bikers settle up and get on their way to wherever.

I move a coaster with two fingers like it's part of an air hockey game. I say to Judson, "Whatever happened with Lacy?"

He rubs the back of his hand across his nose.

I'm hitting the coaster against the bottom of my beer bottle wondering if he's going to respond when he says, "She decided to keep it."

I look back at the red sand shovel left in the ice maker. "You gonna marry her?"

"Who? Lacy? Fuck no. I'm not marrying Lacy. Why would I want to deal with her shit for the rest of my life?"

"So what're you gonna do?"

"Get a fucking lawyer, I guess."

An hour goes by. Judson cuts the air conditioning and has me open up the windows since he's busy mixing mojitos for some out-of-towners who had heard of them on "Sex and the City." They probably aren't great mojitos, but the girls seemed content to pretend. "They're dirty with the satisfaction," he mouths to me while the girls giggle together.

I tilt my head back and smile in recognition.

"When you get a chance, bring me a little more of this High Life, and those green beans. They're great."

He comes back my way, "I know. I grow the beans in an empty lot next to my house then I pickle them here. I use white wine vinegar, onion, garlic, about ten red chilies, some jalapenos, rock salt, and pickling spice. Boil it up. Two weeks in the cellar and they're ready. My grandma used to make a pickle similar to it with all sorts of vegetables but not quite as hot. But I love these with a vodka or Bloody Mary. Nice offset for the flavors."

"You should sell them to all these type of fucks, folks you know. They'd give you a fortune for 'em."

"Not my style. I like the Ball Mason jars. The lids especially. And I like the quiet morning making them couple times a year. I want a tradition, not another job out of it."

Someone puts some money in the old juke box. Jimmy Cliff. Outside, a couple of guys tie a German shepherd to the stop sign and come in for a game of darts. I drink two more beers and watch the dog from the window as the evening moves on. The dog turns his head watching people walk by on the sidewalk. Then he settles down and falls asleep.

Conan has Emilio Estevez on as a guest. The TV's muted so I have no idea what brought Emilio onto a talk show. But his chat washes by with the rest of it.

Then it is just me and Judson.

He says, "You think I'll be a good dad?"

"You know you're gonna be better than mine."

He laughs.

I get off the stool, put the chairs up on the tables, shut the windows, turn off the neon signs, and check the bathrooms for anything vile while Judson cleans up the bar. He lays the stainless steel tools out on a clean towel to dry.

He sets a shot up on the bar, "For your troubles, man. Thanks."

I drink the shot. "No trouble."

He wipes the bar down. He wipes the tables down, wipes the metal work down, tosses the old white towels into the little stainless steel bar sink, fills the sink with cold water, and adds a splash of bleach. He swirls the towels and rinses his hands. "They'll sit over night. You ready?"

JULY & THE BUFF ORPINGTONS

Before their necks are broken they are beautiful. These chickens live under a tent for a week in July. The heat wraps up and around the sides of the tent and hangs thick in the middle. The day is hot but it is hotter inside the tent even with its shade. The bird cages are steel mesh wire. Not big, flimsy hexagons but little, tight squares less than half an inch across. At the places where the wires cross over each other the metal is built up. There is a matte coating over it that hides the welds. Slow, scaly feet move easily over the open-work wires but are careful, intentional.

The fans are humming. They are old and rattling—real metal fans that hang in four corners of the tent. The air is heavy and even these industrial fans are ridiculous against such weight. Smells circulate but air barely moves with the fans' futility. It is so hot for the birds that someone, some thoughtful caretaker, brought a plastic home-use fan. Everyone has a fan like this. It's the kind that sits on dingy golden carpet in hallways, by sunken couches in living rooms, on cherry veneer tables beside beds where love gets made, and on top of endlessly-flashing-noon-'cause-no-one-knows-how-to-reset-the-time microwaves in disinfected kitchens. So, having seen such fans everywhere else, it's not so strange to see one in the poultry tent. Someone has pushed the darkest brown button and pulled the white peg up so the fan will oscillate on top of the middle row of cages. As the fan directs and redirects its effort, pink, purple, blue, and white ribbons sing out, fluttering enough to draw attention to particular cages. Those wire rooms for the birds are lined up as a single-file perimeter around the sides of the tent and two deep back-to-back down the center. Observers flow as if channeled through thick-walled ventricles of a heart.

Feathers move slightly as the fans push the air. There are bits of feathers gathered down around the wooden stilt-legs of the cages on the limestone gravel. There are feathers in the fans. And feathers in the cages. And feathers in the taut fraying jute ropes of the tent. Just downy white and gray pieces mostly. The few good, big, pretty, golden feathers are picked up quickly and swept away to shaft-stroking wonderlands with the giggles of little girls.

The chickens pick up their bony, intentional feet and slow-dance, sometimes even with flapping wings. They turn and their feet seem backwards. Then, not forgotten, the bodies turn. With short jolts, their heads betray nothing held in confidence. The eyes focus and then turn away. Strangers read names of the owners out loud and point, showing each other whatever they see as important. We do it, too. "Come over here and look at this one."

For twenty years my mother has taken me and my father to the fair. We go through the sheep barn. We go through the cattle barns, dairy and beef. We look up at the names painted on the rafters: names of friends, and brothers of friends, and fathers of friends. Green paint on old white paint. We remember our head, our heart, our hands, and our health. Sandals fill with dust as we walk down the missing-lightbulb midway. We eat something familiar because it's only once a year. There is no anxiety for goldfish swimming through food-color-dyed waters in dirty bowls and no mortal fear for the cheap stuffed nothings everyone wants to win.

We wander slowly through it all. It is hot, July. We stop. I want to watch the boys throwing darts at a rainbow wall of slack balloons. Because there is no sense of impending doom for that child who paid for his three chances. He aims while my father crosses his arms over his chest and stares. We feel the imminent impact. We want the child to perform well, to win the biggest, best prize: the huge stuffed tiger. But who can really hope for so much? And what responsibility does this child have to our family? None. So. We don't really care if the child bursts something nothing-filled. We don't expect it. The first dart glances off the pulverized wooden board and drops into a metal collecting tray. He refocuses. Aims again. Then one, two steel darts pop big yellow flopping balloons as we cheer, congratulate, and smile. The child turns to us and smiles too. Dad walks on. We follow.

It cannot be that this will kill him. I look at my father, who stands with us eating a pork burger from the Rotary Club's tent. He watches the people walk by. He speaks to the ones he knows. They don't know yet, but we know. And still we smile and say hello. We laugh at the round-bellied kid in the little red tee shirt. And we ask the questions that you ask. But we don't say, "He's dying." We will have to soon enough.

We walk through the barns where my projects once were. Barns I remember cleaning on cold spring days when you shouldn't really use a hose yet. Barns I remember hiding in. At five and fifteen. They still smell the same. Hay. Dirt. Sunshine. Cement. And Time. No one savors moments like this, moments when you share personal speculations about who will probably win in all the baked goods categories. So. We wander over to the show ring.

The hogs fill up the arena. We laugh at the smallest children showing the comparatively huge animals. They rush around the ring in their little Wranglers, boots, and tucked-in dress shirts. But we don't laugh at their age or stature. We laugh in appreciation of their competence. They know everything about showing hogs: shine them; tap them with the little whips; keep the hogs between their bodies and the judges; move the animals along quickly so their ears flop and their haunches bounce on coquettish trotting hooves; and always keep both eyes right on that judge.

We all fall in love with one tiny skinny boy in particular, because he's so focused, so intent, so practiced, so self-assured, so competitive.

He will grow up here, that boy showing those hogs. Knowing how. But we all grew up here. Not Mom. Not Dad. But the rest of us. The woman leaning over the fence grew up here. The man sitting next to me grew up here. I grew up here.

And so I know everything that happens in this ring. There are auctions. There are dances. There are obstacle course races where greased-up kids hold greased-up watermelons and go under bales of hay, through kiddie pools of water, and shimmy around poles to ride scale-model tricycle-tractors towing stacked cinder blocks on skids. Fair queen pageants go on here where girls win and girls lose. But today it is the hogs oiled up and glittered in the ring looking very good and showing off.

The judging is over and there won't be anything else going on in the ring for a while. So we head back towards the car but stop. Mom wants to walk through the poultry tent. So we do. The birds are preposterous. They are amazing forms of life. They are beautiful and clean and cocky. Before their necks are broken.

She never asked to move here.

"The Buff Orpingtons are my favorite," she says. She holds his hand. And she knows that he's dying. And she knows the chickens are dying. And she was still careful to park in the shade in July.

CONVERSATIONS IN SILENCE

Do you wake up blaming an insidious enemy for your flailing arms, blind aggression, and sweat? Do you wake up in a place unable to cope, understanding that some enemies never show their faces, would rather die than let you have a chance at a fair fight? I hate these demented shadows we cast ourselves with paranoia, self-doubt, and fear. I don't know if we hide them or they hide us. You're you, Daddy, but where's the dignity gone?

We are combatants, but how? Integrity, autonomy, and free will; my God, what transient jokes. Those shadows cower even if we won't succumb. There's no definitive mark of the divisions between us, between you now and who you once were. I don't know what you call our overlap—solidarity, communion? Or. Just call it a lifetime of memory. And give me some image to assign to these few shared successive hours. I don't care what image. A photo album will work. An old reel of 8 mm film will work, too. Or, yes, sure, a little postcard, a painting of seagulls dive bombing for breakfast. Yes, that will definitely work. Wedge it in the bathroom mirror frame. Forget about it. No. Don't. Please don't, ever. I don't care. Not everything can be objectified. Just hand me a father to have forever when arbitrary things like misinterpreted train schedules force submission.

But. Take all of that, that whole thing, and wrap it into one big image. Something enough, you know. Something bold and beautiful for both of us. Like maybe there's some kind of skyward woman. Yeah. Grace of not-God. Not a ghost. Not a mermaid. But more than an apparition she is out somewhere in the fields singing to herself with everything you never told us. She is limber in her work and asks only for rain. I don't know who she is. You never really said. But I don't need to question things that help. What I know is, when she's here, with you, with me, the wraiths recede. They go as soon as they hear her mandolin.

And so what if anyone knows my father is not my father anymore—except that he is, but changing.

Just after dark, on a bike, in September trees seem whiter than black but fading. We cannot wait to get past the present. Except that then he will be gone. There will be only photo albums. No 8 mm reels of film. No big, beautiful skyward woman. So I am coming home to be there, readied for the grief. I sort memories. There are backyard memories, kitchen memories, piano bench memories, Dairy Queen memories, hallway memories, front yard memories, memories from his work, memories from my school. Finally I walk into the bedroom, Mom and Dad's bedroom, and find a few accessible memories there. With one foot on the floor, asleep before dinner, Dad is stretched out on his back taking a nap in the half-light. Thousands of times he lay like this. His image is etched somewhere deep in the everyday meld of what seems right, good, and just. I will never see him that way again. The house is sold.

I hear her holler from the fields, "Keep it in the same tense, Missy." And I laugh as the time twists over its Möbius swirl. It is all now and all removed from time as well. He is lying on the bed at home. He is lying on the couch. He is lying on the cot at Riverhead. He is lying on the floor in the living room. You say they are memories. And so be it. But what part of life would you choose to be most vivid when he is lying in a nursing home, dying? The past is certainly present; it's what I choose.

I hate to think you wake up unsure. Do you know what is happening, Dad? You must try something. At least blame an insidious enemy for your flailing arms, blind aggression, and sweat. Sometimes I sit here, seven hours apart, thinking of you there, in that chair that gets sterilized twice a day. But then I think of you there in the orange chair in the living room at home or sitting in a chair at our kitchen table grading papers. You had slow times then, didn't you? So that eases the burden of how slow your time is now.

She strums a G chord. "Keep it in the same tense, Missy."

It is tense.

For some reason, the idea of your dying bothers me less than the fact that you will never again pour a bowl of Cheerios, top it with Quaker Honey Granola, two spoons of sugar, and milk. You will never have a dripping nose while shoveling snow in the driveway. You will never raise your eyebrows and smile after tickling my feet. You will never stand between me and the television at the most crucial point in a plot. You will never stamp your feet inside the door after coming in from the weather. You will never look skyward through countless vultures spiraling down on an updraft while driving seventy miles per hour on the interstate. You will stop looking for a Cooper's hawk up high.

How long the days seem to me sitting here, seven hours apart. No one talks about distance anymore. Everything's a matter of time travel. There are silent conversations we all have with each other, with the wraiths, with the big, beautiful skyward women. Those conversations are just prayers, I guess, requests for understanding, dreams of being understood. I remember several days after the snows a mess of thistle seed and tiny sparrow foot prints at the base of the backyard feeder. The light was heartening. Do you remember when you cut the tops of the spruce trees for our Christmas trees? Those strange trees. In that morning snow light over thistle and sparrow footprints.

They say it's not really genetic.

That maybe you soaked it in. There are your hands in the lamplight, the veins and tendons and length. Do you think this disease came from those years of washing your hands in the formaldehyde that brought corpses to the lab? I remember you laughing, scaring me by pulling a dead cat up out of a plastic barrel. There must have been fifty dead cats in there all submerged in preservative. You probably shouldn't have just stuck your bare hand in there like that. It's that kind of thinking that brings the wraiths.

So I stare like you taught me to stare. And she is there again, singing. She is bent over her work and dutiful to the land. She pulls and works the fields. And she does not mind. And she knows what I never will know about you. She must. Someone must. You cannot go without someone knowing. Who is she? Who have you told your stories to, Daddy? Where can I find her?

But she's not telling. She sings, "Come and follow me. I'll make you worthy. Come and follow me. I'll make you fishers of men."

They say people, place, or thing. Fine. And the people hurt. And the places hurt. And things hurt. Your bird books. Your telescope. Your driving lessons. Your camera. Thoughts of your lawn-mowing shoes and red Heifer Project International hat. Your black socks. Your watch. Your desk chair. Those great scissors in your desk drawer. The tools. The shed. The paint. All of it. All of the integuments we knew of you.

I imagine you so often. Awake and afraid. Asleep and unknowing. A moment of awareness and more and more hours of nothing.

They told me the name of this thing you have, as if it mattered, as if I might want to know what exactly was happening and how.

If it were anyone else, I would have looked it up.

Give him a break, God. Let him be spared too much. Wherever he is, let him hear birds and see wildflowers in the ditches along the way. Make his journey quick. Do not betray him. He has worshipped this world's beauty for seventy years. Let him be. Give him his freedom. Give him his peace. Give him his dignity back in our memories. Let him be. Just leave him alone. Leave him alone.

And yet I laugh at that phrase. Our culture's most protective phrase is so devastating. "Leave him alone." We jump to the defense, but what do we say? We say, "Leave him alone." Where is the hope of a connection? Where is the promise of a relationship? Where is the unified front? It must not be. Leave him alone. The most courageous phrase we can utter is for another to be left and to be the only one around.

So true underneath. So horrible in the living out.

But She is there, Dad. Don't worry. She is waiting with some kind of release. She sings and mends her nets. She works the fields of the sky and undoes the doing up. She must not be afraid, like I am. She must not be buried alive by this, like I am. She must already know. So I trust her. I have to. Become your own time of *leave him alone*. Become your own beautiful way. And even if I'm left alone I will be with you tiling the floors, painting the doorjambs, picking out Christmas trees, sweeping the gravel off the driveway, trimming the juniper bushes, and watching so many birds fly.

VARIANCE

Men vary. There are those who move into this world with a blithe confidence. And there are those who, like myself, are weary at the neck of the hourglass.

I'm waiting for my lover in the pebbled courtyard of our fifth-favorite restaurant. We chose it not because it's cheap but because it's close to his work.

I hate iconic, banal shit like my father's dying. Part of me even hates this May blue sky.

I am aware of my own presence so much sometimes. It's like I'm here, I'm me, but I'm also this self-consciousness, this constant kind of correction. Self-control. Self-discipline. Self-awareness. All of it right here under this pecan tree. And not only here. Everywhere I go it goes—walking, working, even going home. Especially going home. I just keep cutting away what's unacceptable and expressing what others will tolerate, can handle, will accept, will love—well, will at least not criticize.

Today is a clean day that makes you want ice water and a swim of absolution. Above me—not just me—there is one of those full blue skies that you always want to remember in November.

On days this gorgeous it seems possible to capture the beauty of that kind of atmospheric blue. Wouldn't it be nice to keep some bit of it, some twist, some lovely description of the sky, some transcendent pleasure that transports you deeper, further, and with ease? Go ahead and try. Try to keep some of the sky for days when crappy gray cloud cover obscures the light. You won't possibly be able to remember this much blue. You cannot hold any great sky in your mind for long. The frustration of the attempt is too much. In November you'll just get pissed off doing your best to envision a May sky.

Don't bother with any duality of the material and the mind. What's the point? Let the blue sky go. Get rid of it. Get rid of it and the memories of your dad listening to The Allman Brothers Band in the basement. Get rid of the lyrics that keep coming back: *Turn your love my way.*

Don't do it. Don't let him win. Don't let the world's pressure separate you from who you are. Hold on.

Stay here. Don't give up. Not again. Even if you were the second inadequate person in your father's righteous world.

The blue sky is unrelated to the material you and unrelated to your dealing with your immaterial dead dad shit. Grief is nothing. Your father's dying without knowing the real you is nothing. It does not matter.

Prove it?

Fine. But can it be done? Can any of this leftover love-like destruction be rationalized?

Because first off: The lovely, spring blue sky is not unrelated to material you because you're breathing it; you're alive inside of all that air. Fine. So. There's a real interaction there that cannot be denied.

Secondly: That May blue heaven is not unrelated to immaterial you because the color of the sky affects your mood. It lifts your spirits when you're dealing with your dead-dad-grief shit.

Just get over it and cope. Plenty of people have secrets.

And this suffering is only like clothes. So. Get up; put on your shoulds.

Something is in conflict. You're sitting at a table under a pecan tree, the sky is cheering you up, but you shouldn't be cheered up. Press your arm over your eyes. Stay with the appropriate grief that makes you a better person. You need the gravity. You need the sadness. You need the import. There are shoulds for everything, especially now with all this dead-dad-grief shit. Don't you dare feel the wrong emotions right now. This is no time to enjoy the expanse of a blue above and beyond who and what you are.

You most need the situation to make sense. If a tragedy has occurred, it should be tragic. You should feel the tragedy of an unexpected death. Your father's unexpected death is tragic. You should not be filled with joy, with gladness, with thanksgiving, with relief, with finality and freedom. Something is wrong. Amiss.

And don't whisper anything long-suppressed like, *That's what happens when the abuser dies.*

You cannot admit gratitude, satisfaction, glee, or any spirit of karmic vengeance. That would be wrong. And yet. What you feel is that whole fantastic May blue sky filling you with renewed life.

You smile your liberated loneness into the blue, alert and ready to wipe that smug smirk off your face if the waiter walks by. And you should do it now anyway because your partner will be here soon. He won't understand if you're sitting there all giddy, happy, and free. So. Sit up. Stop gloating about your well-deserved freedom under the big blue sky. Just be glad, proportionally glad, that it's not tropically humid today. That the air is easy. And that you are no longer alone dealing with your dead-dad grief shit. You're you. A person who can say to himself: *I'm waiting to meet my lover here.*

With confidence even. Or could. Probably.

Probably could.

Definitely. Sure.

River pebbles are the floor of the courtyard and square stepping-stones make a path for the waitress to make her rounds like a geisha bending her head to miss pruned cherry branches burdened with their blossoms. The tables are old iron and glass. The menus are beautiful, written in an almost illegible script. The fountain makes it difficult to eavesdrop. The wine is white and doesn't mind at all.

He'll be late.

So you have time to recover and find yourself again in the moment.

Take the pill. At least take half of it.

Don't you realize? You're the first person now.

And, yeah, I'm glad to be back in New Orleans. There is a lady dressed in a bright pink Irish linen dress and a broad white hat walking two greyhounds. They are like deer and stop to stare at me through the cast iron fence. She moves on easily and they follow, leaving the good restaurant smells behind. The gentleman at the corner table chews his cigar and snaps a newspaper in reaction to an editorial. A waitress appeases him with an artichoke and watercress salad. He puts the paper away and thanks her. "Thanks." The cigar, not quite out, lies forgotten in an ashtray. The smell reminds me of my uncle, my father's older brother who shook uncontrollably, silent through the funeral.

But I'm not home anymore. I'm here where two sisters celebrate a thirty-something birthday with too many drinks in the afternoon. They don't usually drink in the afternoon, you can tell. They probably don't usually drink at all. But it's a thirty-something birthday and so the table rattles between the slipping elbows and the patio stones. They laugh easily and look alike when they do.

Shadows dance across the white napkin in my lap. The leaves of the pecan tree are high above my head, so the shadows are subtle; the grays smudge into each other. Their dance is a flirtation with the wind and falls into my napkin. Half an alprazalam half an hour ago helps sooth the shadows. And I succumb.

"Have you decided?" She is beautiful like a raven on a glacier in the sun. And I cannot look at her. She is a dancer just getting through school with this job. We've spoken before. She knows my friend—my partner, my lover: well, I guess he is my friend—better.

"No. I'll just wait to order. Except for a smidge of spaghetti. Can I just have some plain noodles on a fancy tiny dish with a little pesto? Call it a salad and forgive me."

"Sure." She fills up the water again. "Are you doing okay?"

I smile.

And she gives up. "More wine?"

"Bring the rest of this bottle and chill another. He'll be here soon."

The gentleman in the corner decides on dessert. It seems he has opted out of the main course in order to spend his calories on a piece of pie. Good decision.

A couple, tourists, are seated between me and the fountain. I was watching the fountain so now I am watching the tourists. They are looking around. Looking up at the pecan tree. Looking up at the striped awning that sags over the entry to the courtyard. Looking over at the antique ironwork fountain. Looking at the tiles on the restaurant walls. Looking at the detail in the cast iron fence—cattails and rushes as would surround a stream. Looking at the ironwork of the tables which are frogs bounding up and down splashes of water. Looking at the flagstones and pebbles and the beautiful raven waitress who takes them their water. The lady has cellulite on her thighs and wears comfortable socks. The man is wearing a French Quarter hat that he likely just bought today. They are the explorers of our time. Pacific and glad someone has done it all before. But they are humbled by decision-making. They share one menu. Sweetly.

There is sun in my wine. But I don't care. I drink it anyway.

She brings me my little dish of spaghetti. It looks like a sundae. There is spaghetti in a fancy tiny bowl with a tablespoonful of pesto and a cherry tomato on top. She smiles. And I have to admit it's hilarious. But thank God she understands.

Simplicity is a comfort. Familiarity is a friend. The food is a friend. The smell of the cigar is more than a friend, is family. The tourists taking it all in is a comfort. It's good to be home.

Well. Back from home.

He comes through the side gate. "How was the flight?"

It's funny to look at another individual—about whom you know everything, whom you know better than yourself—in public sometimes. Some intimate lives don't translate easily into communal spaces. All that self-correction comes back: Don't stare. It's not polite. But instead of loving no person more and cleaving to this one man with a whole heart, sometimes it's almost as if you don't feel anything, don't care, don't even know the man at all. You sit there together without your tangible connection, like business associates or brothers if you're lucky. But intellectually you know something real exists, even if it's immaterial.

What, if anything, is love? There must be a reason he came and sat down with you, here, at your table. So your years are built on faith as much as anyone's and without touching anything, not hands, not arms, not legs, not thighs, not lips, no part of the material you, he still reaches in and you remind yourself: *This man is yours forever.*

"Fine. The flight was fine."

"Sorry I wasn't there."

"How's work?"

"Please don't do that."

The waitress approaches him with a kiss on each cheek. His suit is navy and the lining opens up to her. She pours him water and a glass of the wine. They chatter. Then they remember that today shouldn't really be a blue sky day in May. I wish they hadn't remembered my dead-dad-grief shit. Just keep chattering.

And I can tell he doesn't want to deal with the somber reality any more than I do. He invites her to sit down. He never was that intimate. Especially not with the big stuff.

Who is?

She is, that arctic goddess, not Norwegian but Icelandic. She's got the whole thing down pat. She puts the pitcher down, puts her hand on my shoulder, squats in all those shifting shadows, and says to me, "How's your mom holding up?"

I say something back that makes her stand up quickly and go away. A cocktail of finesse, tenuous anxiety, morbidity, and peevishness—she needs to be busy explaining the menu to the tourists anyway.

My lover's not pleased with the way I treated his friend. With his eyes he says my behavior's inexcusable even under the circumstances. But what he actually says is, "Do you want to go away this weekend?"

"I just got home."

"I know. But do you want to go away this weekend?"

And so it is that faith is unnecessary again. There is real love. There is a true connection. And he does understand, completely. He knows everything that's worth knowing about whatever it is that's me. He cares. He shouldn't but he does. And he is strong in the midst of all the impossibilities of it. He exhales suddenly and puts his hand on my thigh.

The tears affect my view of the tourists so I blink them away.

"How did he look?," he asks.

It's hard to say. "He looked—less."

"Yeah."

I bend over and put my forehead against the cool glass tabletop. The tears come quickly. I pick up a handful of the river pebbles and fend off the banged-up basement memories. The rocks slip through my fingers.

"What are you doing with those rocks?" He is laughing and a little uncomfortable. I wish he weren't so uncomfortable. He has a lot of insecurities. He looks from side to side to see if anyone is bothered. But I know and trust the people at the other tables. They're all right. They didn't care when I did what I had to do to block out the penetrating joy of a May blue heaven.

He puts his hand in the middle of my back. I hate that. I like it on one side or the other but not the middle. Why do people do exactly what you hate and exactly what you wish they wouldn't right when you need them to do the right, best thing? Strange. A distancing thing, I suppose.

Awareness. Come closer. Get closer. Or you will drift—safe, calm, away, and done (who cares?)—into some lone forever. Get closer. Do it now. Reach out. Don't descend. Say it. Say to your lover—the man who asked you a thousand times to be truthful, to include your family in your life, to be proud of him, of yourself—say, "I'm sorry. I'm just so fucked up."

He will never really forgive you. But he says, "It's okay. He was your dad."

There's no other. There is a breeze and I don't want anything from anyone under this happy full blue sky. I don't want anyone to turn his love my way. So with one jolt of my thigh I jerk his hand off. I interlace my fingers behind my head like my dad used to do, lean all the way back in the chair, and look up. The pecan leaves dance wildly for just a moment in some small way, some impossible way. They are almost free but exist attached, like all of us bound to this life for as long as possible. They shake and tear at their foundation but never break free. Until it is time. It isn't time now. And when it is time they won't be ready and they will regret this violent shaking in the wind trying to rid themselves of exactly who they are, in some pecan-leaf way.

PORTRAIT OF A WHEEL SPOKE BLUR

An old woman made her yarn on useless beach house days.

Rhythm rain. Rhythm heartbeat. Rhythm breath and blinking. Her foot worked the pedal. Rhythm rain, breath, and wooden pressing rubber down. Inside on the porch during the rain her hand held a strand between two old purple-veined fingers, rolling, twisting, holding the newly-made thread out at a full arm's length, and on a spool spun dandelion-dyed woolen-stretched rhythm and wooden pressing rubber down.

But. That's later. First the old lady picks through the wool loosening the fibers, getting rid of any debris.

The waves and seasons and tides moved on. Spring tide. Neap tide. The sun and moon came to her porch painted gray. Under the privacy blinds sea treasure

that little hands had run offering and wondrous for
generations covered low bookshelves that somehow held
up under the weight of so many lives lost. Among them a
horseshoe crab, a ten-inch whelk, and an elegant, black,
desiccated pouch of skates' eggs. Sea glass rescued and
reclaimed sat amidst this happy desolation that ocean-edge
collectors find so soothing. No one walking on a beach—
looking, searching, hoping—thinks much of dead droves
of sea creatures or of the churning, sandy, blasting hell
where sharp brokenness is pummeled to nothing. No.
Beachcombers seek only perfection.

Children built her house. Such children had gone
off and come back parents and grandparents. And on the
smooth wooden painted floor this great-
aunt/grandmother/mother/sister/ daughter/wife's pedal
hit in quiet rhythm with wooden pressing rubber down,
and rhythm afternoon slant light, and blackberry-stained
ghosts spinning down the beach from Penny Rock and
Briar Croft, with their headless chickens to scald, and their
dead footstep rhythm pressing memories down from Mile
Rock to Port Jeff.

Perfection. Uniformity. What nonsense and bother
for a woman who raised five kids under the moon and
sun's tense constant dance of evasion. Why worry? Just

make enough yarn for all the sweaters, all the hats, all the knitted winter days.

During her breaks she handed out sandwich cookies from special kitchen jars and was part of three hundred familial years on that land against water. She could laugh, joke, carry on, and tell stories until no one could breathe. Old ladies don't smell like smoke anymore. But with that strand of wool held out at arm's length and that pedal working over and over and over and over she focused on nothing but uniformity. The pedal hit the hollow wooden porch floor. And the waves hit the pummeled-nothing sand. And the heat hit the middle-of-nowhere house roof. And the steel flag clips hit the factory-made pole. And the bottom of the sailboat hit her gravelly stretch of beach, got pulled up above the endless tide line through innumerable pre-sorted, shell-marked graves. And the rubber-edged garage door pressed down softly against moss and evening as it ended her driveway.

She was caught spinning and was rhythm witness to summer migrations. Rolling the thread up with two fingers and dropping that spindle again she fed clouds into simple machines after all the required rhythm to tease and coax oily wool—full of seeds and twigs and leftover sheep curls—into something useful.

She lay some fiber on the bed of nails. It's called carding. Have you seen it done? Imagine holding two pet-grooming brushes, one in each hand, used to pull hundreds of slight-bent wires across each other and across the wool. Over and over and over and over those wiry cards with handles got caught in each other's grip as her wrists flicked, her hands flipped, and the wires yanked through a woolen puff until every tangled twist let go. A childhood friend might ask why. The old lady in her housecoat all zipped up modest and warm would answer, "So the little hairs all go in one direction."

The kids never told.

On the deck, where flag shadows flapped on sunny days, the gray paint was hotter than such a light color should be and rhythm feet ran up from their swims, from their high-tide screaming cannonballs off barnacled jetties and their 9.5-rated Olympic swan dives off smooth-topped granite boulders into her jelly fish-strewn seaweed waves. She didn't have to look up and look out to see all the cousins swarming Dragon Rock and racing to find Swim. She heard those children playing safe in the warm rain. She heard their rhythm laughter as they ran like a troupe of high-wire performers through beach grass along the blistering creosote-coated bulkhead. She heard their plans to sneak up the cliff through wild roses. She heard them chase, race, and pant at the hose rinsing off sandy feet before daring to come inside onto her crewel rugs.

Rhythm witness the slow heat of afternoon sleep. Wakeful but dreaming. She didn't care how many little eyes watched the wheel go round or the wooden pedal pressing rubber down over and over. Rhythm dunk lift and twist in the dandelion dye. Rhythm dunk lift and twist all the wool-washing kinds of preparation that she did out back in big steel pans of blue borax water nested in deep, cool shaded sand near a feeder for birds. Just like she did to rhythm dunk lift and twist ten swim suits at the end of the day. Tart lemonade refreshed burnt-skin children that stood watching the sun catch slow drips off the row of hung-up suits. Rhythm breath and blinking.

Huge screens inhale and exhale on maybe-a-storm's-coming breeze. Warblers pretend to be lost in the grapevine. The smell of sandalwood drifts through the slow-tossing briar and locust brambles as does the sound of laughter. Some loved ones are playing cards.

Up and down stairs. Up and down suns. Up and down flags. Up and down drop-spindle, round and round wooden wheel, spinning on, making wool, making sweaters, making blankets, making hats, making mittens, making gloves, making scarves, making socks, making enough layers to keep us all cozy. She was rhythm witness and a BLT; one blue foot on top of the other in the kitchen. Emphysema laughing over on you, holding your arm—with strong, strong hands.

EVE

I almost couldn't bear to watch what I knew was coming.

She's growing up fast but you can only learn so much in twenty-six months. When it was over, and it was over so quickly, she just screamed in agony—cried out with her knowing—until I rushed over and grabbed her up off the floor.

"Oh. My sweet baby girl."

Five minutes before I did, I just waited and watched while she discovered her world. I could hardly breathe. But I knew I had to let her do it.

From a doorway, or a window, I guess, one may look in upon a child, playing alone. One thinks of white canvas, and rain. Her room's too much like a doll's house with one side open to the world. She is there *in toto*: Wrist.

Neck. Little folds of skin. Fingers. A big toe folded against the floor. Head tilting—thought and compassion. Before words. Before all the many words, she is there taking it in.

The doll, another American Girl, is ragged with insipid eyes worn thin from bathing. Her stringy plastic hair is pretend-brushed. Her dress is smoothed by awkward fingers. How can anyone be expected to grip a soft plastic foot with its molded toenails, to let a favored toy girl flop backwards upside-down with her hair hanging, and climb, careful-toddler climb, up onto the window-seat toy box? But my daughter did it and relegated the doll to its little blue plastic rocking chair near the plant on the broad sill.

Ambivalent and then decided she went down again. A toy car drove through a wooden maze of forgotten blocks.

Needing it. Having to have it. She grabbed a book. Upside down. Sideways. Right side up. The fermented paper pages were yellowed and old and must have felt scratchy to little fingers, always learning. It is a golden-spined book called *The Seven Little Postmen* about one special letter they each carry for a distance through wind and rain and driving snow.

But as the sun streams in, she tires. She lies down on her belly. Her fingers touch the carpet. For the nursery my husband insisted on Berber with two layers of the thickest padding underneath. So my baby girl lolls on that nice floor her daddy made her and the hand goes over and over the places her fingers can reach without stretching before it slows. The little fingers rest easily against the knots in the fabric of a pillow lying on the floor nearby. And she is still for a moment.

The room slows. I look up and gaze around the room. It seems the toys watch over her. Outside the window summer hits glass like a starling stunned and the elm tree shades that side of the house. I look down at my daughter again. She's almost asleep with her little cheek resting against the nubby floor.

I was about to turn and go. Then her head sprang to attention. Again desire. Total focus on something that must have rolled under the rocking horse. And I'm riveted with her in the moment. She wants it. She crawls around. She slides under. She throws out blind hands. Not quite. She tries again. Still she cannot reach it. So she gets up and drags the stumbling rocking horse back enough to go in underneath and push out her find.

Kaleidoscope. And sunshine through the other window.

She is on her back. Her feet are in the air. They wriggle. Now they rest on the rocking horse where stirrups are painted. Now on the pillow, then kicking the floor. And her eye looks in as her little hand turns.

Red. Before she knows the names of the colors they fall over her in their mixed-up rainbows. With that sandy rattle from inside the pretty world turning.

Brilliant yellow.

Blue.

Flowers

And pink.

Enthralled, she laughs out loud.

Uninhibited.

Amazed.

Enraptured.

But curious.

To be in that world. To find one's way into that world. Colors tossing easily and free-falling with shaken, circular gravity into the middle of the world. There is a drunken moment when she believes in the place inside. She wants it.

She takes her eye away. She hits the toy on the floor. Looking in again but her hand covers the aperture and with no light she sees little. She hits it repeatedly on the floor. And again on the rocking horse.

She turns it, looks in backwards, and sees nothing. The world has disappeared. But turning it again the furious rage dissipates; she is satisfied. And she has learned how to hold it up once more towards the light for soothing patterns and a falling sound. Again she is amazed. Enraptured.

But still curious.

She carries the kaleidoscope over to her toy box. Standing up she puts the handle of the toy box lid at such an angle so as to be able to pry the thing apart. She works diligently. Pushing from one side and then on the other. To be inside. To live in that world.

Finally!

A half-smile. She got it.

Then.

Beads hemorrhage for an instant.

Little one-sided plastic nothing mirrors lie motionless.

The cardboard is bland inside the pretty paper.

And I cannot get to her fast enough.

ANGELS ON HORSEBACK

Kitchens breathe easily in big families. There is a blur of aunts and uncles leaning on counters. Teenage cousins avoid obligation in the basement surfacing only to refill a bowl of tortilla chips. Little nephews play with string cheese on the floor. At the end of the kitchen there is an island where neighbors are sitting on bar stools drinking mai tais, white wine, and sangria. They get up to take turns throwing a doll's head (a beloved dog toy) into the living room. Charlie, the golden retriever, bounds back to the slow-swirling group and looks around among different friendly faces before choosing one and offering up his drool-covered prize.

A twenty-six-year-old woman, the new wife of one of the older grandchildren, stands awkwardly apart from the group. The loudest neighbor demands that she come toss the doll's head. She declines but so as not to seem too standoffish she instead makes a large gesture of maturely closing the basement stairs door in an effort to improve her political position in the familial hierarchy. Who does that surly nineteen-year-old think he is to let a door stand open in the middle of the way as he rushes and rumbles down the steps?

But. Who is she to care? So she leans over and picks up the lone tortilla chip he dropped from his refilled bowl lest it get crushed and require whatever reprimand might come out with the vacuum.

Mrs. Hamel from church is carrying serving dishes out to the screened-in porch. She seems never quite pleased with the platters' spacial relations. The buffet under the kitchen window goes through different permutations. Deviled eggs, potato salad, coleslaw, orange Jell-O and carrot salad, teriyaki chicken wings, and mint-frosted chocolate chip brownies dance, leapfrog, slide around, and push back in her old, gnarled, manicured hands until she's satisfied.

No one is listening. But Mrs. Swindan answers what must have been a question posed by that new wife of one of the older grandchildren, "Angels on horseback are just baked oysters wrapped in bacon," then raises her voice to shout toward the porch, "Mrs. Hamel. How do you make your Christmas fruit salad?"

Mrs. Hamel hears the question but doesn't bother raising her voice much. She's folding napkins corner-to-corner and making a pinwheel pile. "The oranges are from Central America. None of this grocery store nonsense. Mine come directly from the grove to my back door. Lord knows what infestations I'm ushering in on the fruit, but I don't care. I'm an old lady, I like good oranges, and I hate pesticides."

When the twenty-six-year-old comes through the doorway carrying the fruit salad, Mrs. Hamel points to one of two empty places of honor, and the prized dish gets turned ninety degrees counterclockwise.

"So you cut the oranges. Lots of them. Let the juice run in too. Then the apples. I like the Gala from Washington State, but you can be more flexible with the apples. Just don't use those big red ones covered in soapy wax from the store. They're mealy and awful. Use a good baking apple over a good lunchbox apple. They won't take on as much fluid and mush down on you. I've even used the Granny Smith. They are tart but firm and get balanced by so much soft sweetness in the salad. The Golden Delicious is fine if you can't find the Gala and don't want the tart zing of the Granny Smith. But the Golden will get soft after a while."

Mrs. Swindan only asked to be polite. She drifts off from the kitchen to get the three-tiered cake plate from upstairs. But. The young woman keeps listening.

Mrs. Hamel folds more napkins. "After the apples go in, squirt it with some lemon juice to prevent all those apples from browning. The orange juice just isn't acidic enough. Then the maraschinos. Halves or quarters, whichever you have time for. Lastly, the coconut. Best to grate it fresh yourself from the meat of a coconut. But I'll admit I've only done that once. It was such a mess getting into that thing! It took a screwdriver and a hammer and a lot of words that I'd rather not employ to get that sucker open. The blessed thing rolled off my counter so many times that I ended up on the floor with it. My legs holding it steady then hacking at it with that screwdriver and hammer. Awful. And the milk got all over my shoes and dress when I finally did get it open.

"So I do recommend the store-bought, fully-processed, shredded coconut. A quarter to half a bag. A good fistful is about right. And really it works out better than the fresh coconut because the dry coconut takes up the maraschino juice and the orange juice for blended flavor. But that coconut is mainly for texture and looks.

You can leave it out if you must. It's a great salad Christmas morning with breads and spreads. Stollen and cream cheese every year at our house." She smiles. "The key is high quality oranges. A definite must. Not worth making with crap oranges."

"Thank you, Mrs. Hamel. Someday I'll try it out."

"Well, not until you tell me how you come up with these beauties year after year." Mrs. Hamel gestures toward the deviled eggs. It's clear enough that Mrs. Hamel hates deviled eggs. But one's recipe is never just given away. It must be exchanged for another equally as good. And everyone says that these particular deviled eggs are as near to perfection as Icarus ever was to the sun, which is much too close for Mrs. Hamel's comfort. She slams the salt and pepper shakers down against the table in three different places. Nowhere seems right.

But. The young wife didn't make the deviled eggs. So she shakes her head and points to a tray of cookies that she only had to bake in ready-made batches for eight to ten minutes. She says she thinks one of the neighbors made the deviled eggs and cranes her neck inside to ask. But the neighbors have their backs turned, still throwing the doll's head, and are also distracted from her uninvolved incursion by watching the middle school boys'

well-matched race in a video game. So the story of the
deviled eggs is never told.

Mrs. Hamel is glad not to have to listen to such rot
about whoever thinks she can make the best plate of
deviled eggs but also demonstrates a sort of disappointed
disgust in the girl's inability to assert herself.

The young new wife of one of the older
grandchildren is not just a girl and doesn't think it is her
fault that the row of neighbors can't hear her asking for
the deviled egg recipe. And why should she interrupt them
when Mrs. Hamel doesn't even want to listen? Still, it's
true enough that she isn't quite sure which one of the
neighbors made them. So there is no one in particular to
ask. She wanders away from Mrs. Hamel, opens the door
to the basement stairs, and disappears.

Back in the kitchen Mrs. Swindan has come
downstairs. She and Mrs. Roth are working away.
"Doesn't it seem unlikely?" Mrs. Swindan says it as if
caught—an eagle in a tall chicken wire fence. A fight is
useless. They are sisters. And so the reply from Mrs. Roth,
"Mmm." She preheats the oven and begins to pour a layer
of rock salt into a jelly roll pan. The sound of the salt
against the metal is muffled by jazz.

The sink is full of ice. The kitchen walls bask in
the last of the afternoon sun. The white wine, in glasses

lined up in the window, holds glimpses of the light. Leaning on the stove, hands on the aprons, sipping periodically, the sisters clean and straighten up nothing that needs to be done. They are waiting for the oysters.

The conversation dies easily. A pattern made by a thousand arguments not bothered with in the presence of guests, like this nosy young wife of one of the older grandchildren. The matronly sisters pretend not to notice that she keeps popping up every time they both turn around. Mrs. Roth might involve her but cannot remember her name. So instead she watches a group of children trample her sugar snap peas in the garden as they squabble about who should retrieve the soccer ball. Her children and her sister's children and some children of friends are trying to be careful, but the soccer ball has wreaked havoc enough.

The peas can handle it. She turns away from the window and tries to remember the name of the young woman Mrs. Hamel must have rebuffed, picks up her glass, and puts the back of her hand against the oven door, testing the heat.

"What's Owen's new wife's name?"

"I thought you knew. She stood there hovering and I had absolutely no idea. I was about to ask."

"Mrs. Hamel must have said something to her. She slithered down the stairs two minutes ago."

"I didn't see that. Are you sure?"

"Yes. You know how she can be."

"Who?"

Mrs. Hamel overhears Mrs. Swindan and Mrs. Roth. She said, "Her name is Christa. And I didn't say a word. The girl's got no—"

But Mrs. Swindan doesn't wait for her comment. She yanks the basement door open. "Christa!"

Christa hurries up the stairs. She stands close to Mrs. Roth who quickly hands her the salad tongs. "Just toss everything together. Be sure to get the tomatoes and olives off the bottom." Mrs. Swindan doesn't bother to remind her sister that three people asked for salad without dressing and that two others hate olives, which is why things were as they were with the dressing on the bottom.

But. Mrs. Hamel forgets nothing. "What do you expect Andre to do?" Christa looks first to Mrs. Roth, who has obviously forgotten, then to Mrs. Swindan, who shakes her head, and lastly to Mrs. Hamel who throws her hands up proving herself beyond all culpability. Christa says, "I'm sorry. I didn't know."

Everyone is relieved by the sound of the garage door rising. Two men laugh heartily. One opens the door.

The other backs his way up the stairs, slowly. They each hold one handle of an old metal tub. They carry it awkwardly through the door and steady it with slow steps, outstretched arms, and dictatorial statements. The women disperse like a flock of starlings that rises just a few feet and settles again on a different part of the lawn. Because they've arrived. Not the men but what they carry.

No one says a word. Everyone watches while the two men lift the tub, tilt it, slowly, slowly. One says, "Steady." And the other wraps his lips around his teeth in a grimace. "Pull it back. Yeah. Okay. Now go." They let the ocean water splash down into the sink. The oysters rattle, clatter, tumble, and fall, piling onto each other in a haze of the sea on ice.

The men tip the tub a few inches further, to be sure, to be absolutely sure. One of them grabs both handles, tips it all the way upside-down to be a hundred percent certain. Mainly for show, the other pounds the bottom of the tub.

But. Though no one expects it, one more oyster, one lodged in the crimp somehow, comes free and drops straight down onto the others.

One of the men says, "That's about twice what we had last year." Satisfied, the men retreat. The tub disappears, gets rinsed, gets forgotten again on the rafters in the garage.

The women do not hesitate to return. They talk and laugh. Their hands are deft as they wield flexible knives.

Mrs. Swindan's nine-year-old son announces, "I want to do one." The young man marries once. And his bride is Impossibility. He conquers her in time. "Let me. Let me try."

His mother hands over her knife. "Find a good one."

The boy takes the biggest oyster he sees.

His mother hands over the glove.

"I don't want to wear that."

"You have to protect your hands. It won't let you cut your fingers off."

The boy reluctantly puts on the wire mesh glove. He holds the oyster level to the ground knowing that the juice will run out if he does not. "Now what?"

"See how it's thicker down here? That's the cup. Across from that there is a sort of hinge. You want to stick the knife right into the hinge. A twist should pop it open and then you cut the bottle muscle."

"I thought it was really hard."

She smiles, knowing. "It is."

The boy, concentrating, holds the oyster with the awkward glove. He finds the hinge and struggles to get the knife tip in. The knife slips and rams into his palm but is stopped by the steel mesh of the glove. His eyes are wide.

"See; we could be on our way to the emergency room right now."

Understanding more, he tries again. He can feel it now. That place where the tip of the knife must penetrate. "I get it." He doesn't falter. The flat tip goes in. He holds the cup firmly but level in the glove and twists his knife hand enough to pop the shell open.

"Now get it loose underneath."

He cuts hesitantly. He doesn't want to lose the juice. He quits, offers up both the knife and the oyster. "I can't. You do it."

"Just keep going slowly. You'll get it."

He does not want to try. He does not want to be told to keep going. He does not want to do it wrong. He does not want to not know how. He keeps looking around, at his mother, at his father, at his aunts, at his dog, at the new wife of one of his older cousins, at his brother, who nods. The pressure of the knife is a little much and the oyster pops back, juice splashing down his wrist, lost. But the muscle was cut and he holds the oyster up so his mother will give it a squirt of lemon juice and a little

Tabasco. He knows this part and sucks it down, relishing his work.

She is satisfied and grants permission for him to be dismissed. He hands back the glove and watches his mother and aunt wield their knives, their experience. They shuck ten to his one oyster and he wonders how it's possible. They shuck them and lay them out on the rock salt without losing a drop of the juice. Even with three-year-olds running past them and tugging at them and screaming at the top of their lungs and crying and fighting over slobbery dog toys. His mother and his aunt don't lose a drop of juice. He is amazed by his mother, but doesn't say so, never will again. And he will forget this moment the instant he leaves the room. Only somewhere—at a funeral, in a boardroom, on a mountaintop—sometime later will the image come back to him and he will be watching again, seeing his mother at the sink shucking oysters.

The oysters marinate for twenty minutes.

But no one waits.

Mrs. Roth goes out to the yard, kicks the soccer ball one time, runs after it, hard, fast, then says nothing but picks up the black-and-white ball and turns back. The children follow her across the lawn, leaping, jumping, trying to grab the ball back before she gets into the house, into the bathroom, where they swarm around her holding their cupped hands up, waiting their individual turns for two squirts of the fun foam soap.

They know the rules. So Mrs. Roth makes no announcement about how the soccer ball will wait in a newspaper basket on top of the TV until everyone's eaten.

Mrs. Swindan can't be bothered right now. She is swirling her hands in the jelly roll pan, smoothing out an inch-deep layer of coarse sea salt. "Just get another bottle from the garage," she says as she scours half the oyster shells and nests them in the salt. Mrs. Roth wraps each fresh oyster in a streaky rasher from the deli downtown and lays it out in a shell. Mrs. Hamel drizzles a mixture of white wine, hot sauce, garlic, and parsley over the shells. Half go out onto Mr. Roth's grill. Half go under the broiler in the kitchen.

The neighbors, talking loudly after all the mai tais, white wine, and sangria, line up, each with a heavy paper plate.

Summer sets in. Mrs. Swindan calls Christa over to the oven. There is no ceremony, no kneeling knightship, no rite of passage for a warrior in the woods, no moment of hesitation at all. Just, "Here. Take this out." So as instructed, the young new wife of one of the older grandchildren carries the most important platter to the table, elbows her way through the line of neighbors, and there are the angels on horseback, between the deviled eggs and Mrs. Hamel's Christmas fruit salad.

DECUSSATION

The river moves midsummer slow. Two poles are forgotten on the weathered wood and three bodies roll naked on a raft, moving over each other but trying not to shift so much they'll all sink. There is no crime where there is an agreement. She moves away from their embrace; lets the men have it for a while. None of them speaks.

Canyon walls rise around the three lovers and their raft floats on the surface of a deep down waterway. She picks up one of the poles, stands, and pushes them further downstream. Granite surrounds whatever questions there are and makes the river seem defined, known, trustworthy in its place. Trees grow on shelves up high and vines hang down from slippery cracks so full of life the rock itself seems to chase hanging algae down its face.

The woman, she's twenty-six, poles over close to one of the river walls, reaches out her hand, and cannot quite touch the rock without affecting their raft's balance. The thick vines droop along the granite, around the saplings on ledges, and she gives up reaching, choosing instead to pull clay from the river's edge onto the raft.

She sits again, lays the pole down, starts rubbing wet clay on one man's legs while he kisses the other.

Warm skin surrounds three minds that are always left untouched like piles of sun-warmed clothes on the bank: a pair of faded, acid-washed jeans; a paper-thin St. Patrick's Day tee shirt; a yellow skirt; two halves of an eight-year-old bikini; a pair of flip-flops; some red shorts; and four forgotten running shoes. All that stuff's left piled together in the woods at the landing by a too-bright yellow Corvette.

They have choices. They aren't children. They each, as consciously as possible, have two more lives taken, and no more longing, no more wanting, no more reasons to wait, to beg, to ask for mercy, to respond, to curl long strands of hair around once-broken fingers and also move whisker-rubbed lips; no, nothing but skin (under a most private sun) rolled respectful of their shared precarious balance, each taken, with rising up, with release, with shifting weight leaning on elbows, on hips, on shoulder blades with arched breast kinds of calling.

The river moves them beyond the canyon into a quiet stand of trees where the waters widen to a knee-deep, nearly-stopped, unhurried serenity. Why talk? There is nothing to say. They forget about conversational formalities, about bellies of laughter, about *tsking* over amnesty for smokestacks, and about who should shamefully have to drag the potted spider plant from room to room.

Someone must.

The one man, the one with clay on his legs, the one who reaches out to the second man with something just beyond brotherhood when he knows that other's gentle heart so desperately, deeply loves him. Neither can do much about his feelings. So one with clay on his legs pulls away from the two strong hands that hold him close. His leaving the caress is something they all notice. With a kind willingness if not with plunging joy he's off the raft and ridding himself of that clay in the water for a minute.

Even with all the maturity of their agreement, the man left with his feelings is not so relaxed. He wants both lovers for himself, now if not forever, and having to share he is angry from the neck up.

She is numb from the waist down. She doesn't love either of them. Not like she should. She lets her legs drag in the cold river water. And she wants to rid herself of knowing either of them. She stands again and pushes the raft downriver. The man left with his feelings stands, too, and picks up the second pole. They move downstream more quickly, more effortlessly, and without the rise and fall that happened when only she was pushing.

But. The man lets go of what's real and picks up what's nonexistent to help propel them all. It's hard for the woman to understand why he keeps making such an effort. But he does. He's working diligently at something she doesn't understand. He kneads what's in front of them with yearning, longing, love, and his twin pangs of hope and despair, sweetness and embittered grace.

There is an elegance as though he wants to draw them more near to something impossible. She turns her mind away from his work and keeps pushing her pole into the river bottom.

The man in the water notices none of the others' unseen exertion and swims behind them both, holding onto the edge of the raft, kicking out with fun frog-legs, blowing bubbles, pushing them all downstream his way, keeping his distance, waiting a few more minutes to get back on.

She likes that he's pushing, helping her make them go, because she doesn't like that—doesn't understand why—the other man laid down his pole and just gave up. The reflections she gathers up from the water exist almost, but they aren't real enough to distract her from the work that's necessary: pulling the pole up, planting it into just a reach ahead, pulling her body closer to that place, bringing the raft along with her feet until her body is past that pole, and then methodically pulling it up, and dipping it again, sometimes twisting from one side of the raft to the other to keep their heading.

The man on the raft is still angry from the neck up. He doesn't understand why they don't know he's laid down the pole and picked up the current instead. Hand-over-hand he pulls the nothing rope that's frayed and twisted as if caught in the teeth of a gar that swims through the shallows of a faraway, nearly unimaginable delta, through brackish silt avoiding the sea. The man left with his feelings on the raft just wants the man in the water to love him; no, not only him, her too. So of course he lays down his pole and pulls the invisible rope and so they move forward. Hand-over-hand the blisters rise. He is pulling them toward an open end where the river gives up like Sunday afternoon onto the flat forgotten parts of the Gulf and they will be there, soon maybe, if he keeps ever-pulling.

Hand-over-hand he is angry from the neck up. Pushing her pole into the mud she ignores his pouting pathos and looks back at the man in the water blowing bubbles, kicking with fun frog-legs. She watches him and he likes it. He notices her gaze and rolls onto his back to let go a belly of sunlight warmth. He wears the silver river lining like a glass ornament blown full of mercury and rises endlessly against impossibility.

She wants him, puts the pole down, starts to climb into the water, but he comes up to her instead, pulls himself onto the raft. With water sheeting down his body and the clay gone he lies in the center of what they've lashed together. They aren't quite callous that the other man pulls them hand-over-hand toward the delta with his whole mind and heart. They just make their love like joint checking used to be.

The man making love to her thinks, "You can love her. Or you can know. But you can't love her and know. It's too much." So he pretends he knows. It's enough.

But the man pulling them all toward an open end with a nonexistent rope made of what's felt is exhausted. It is not quite an interruption of their union when he says, "I'm hungry," as he pulls and pulls and pulls. But he gets tired, bored, lonely, sad, and ties a knot in the rope no one can see.

The other two know he is angry from the neck up.

Agreement or not, the unforgiving middle of a heart cannot be quieted. They do not ignore him but do not include him either and their sweat comes together in places to trickle down off their backs past the hairs and over the muscles.

The other clenches his cringing repetitive curse. "I'm hungry."

Between kisses, between dives, twists, caresses, and unfolded origami car commercial double magazine pages one of the two of them acknowledges him with minimum courtesy, "We know. God, we know."

His bare feet are burning. He wonders about the knot that holds them there being beaten by the sun.

CREPE MYRTLE & SUMMER CICADAS

I am with my husband, who has the day off. It may seem a comfort. Melodious wind and tension left in the sky. But these are delirious times. And electricity doesn't mix well with water.

We've come to the swimming pool after a thunderstorm. My husband does not swim. He has his reasons. I wouldn't say he doesn't want to be here. But coming to the pool today was my idea.

Years ago someone put a lot of thought into this apartment complex. It's got to be older than I am. I don't know. Maybe it's not. Maybe it just needs to be taken care of a little bit better. A little gazebo full of mailboxes has a sturdy wooden floor under which possums must congregate. But anyway the speed-bumped drive is flanked first by flags and then by unambitious trees that grow up any way in raised planters made of railroad ties. Each gray-and-maroon-painted apartment building has a foundation among hardwoods and the swimming pool sits serene amidst them all on landscaped embankments. Crepe myrtle, boxwood, and Bill's Blue deodar cedar nearly strangled by the smilax that's been left untended for years.

The birds are quiet now, just after midday, just after the thundering rain. But the incessant sound of cicadas reminds us of the surrounding heat, which makes the pool road's sloped asphalt seem a steam plate. It is silly to bring a towel to lie on because the chaise lounges are pooled with water. But habits die hard. The sky is still black with clouds. There is the stench of Banana Boat sunscreen but that may be a film on the water.

My girlfriends say my husband's controlling.

We've been talking about it. Not what my girlfriends say. They don't understand him like I do. What I meant is, we've been talking about my wanting to come to the pool today. I thought it would be something fun for us to do on his day off. I didn't think he'd be playing poker online all morning, drinking all the milk, and then keeping at that computer stuff while we waited two more hours for the rain to stop.

I was watching talk shows in the living room but saw him go and get the emergency credit card that's taped to the wall behind the calendar. He took it with him into the back bedroom and shut the door. I heard the lock click. What am I gonna do? Go back there? Try to get the credit card away from him? Try to unplug the computer, turn off the power strip, change his password, tip the monitor over? I've tried all that shit before. What's the point? All he's gonna do is shove me out of the room and get back on that stupid website. No use having that lady upstairs call the cops again. It's not like I care. He's the one who said we needed to only use the credit card for emergencies and keep it taped to the wall and hidden like that. He can do what he wants.

I thought maybe we'd go to breakfast or out to the mall and then talk and laugh by the pool and then make dinner together and make love all night. But once he's on that computer there's nothing I can say. Plus, he didn't want to go to breakfast or out to the mall. Said we didn't have the money. He said we were going to Sonic or staying home, said he always has Sonic for dinner on his days off, said I should know that by now. But I didn't want Sonic. I wanted to make dinner at home. He said, "Fine. Then make dinner. If you don't want to go out and spend more money I don't have, great. Why are we even talking about this?" I am definitely not making love with him after he kept the volume up all the way on his poker game when I was trying to hear my aunt on the phone. So coming to the pool is probably our only fun thing together for his day off, now, and he won't even get in the water with me. He can pretend all he wants but I know he's not asleep over there.

I dive in and split a limpid box full of wet blue that I wish were cooler.

For five minutes, I've got the pool to myself and my husband has all of the deck chairs since it just stopped raining. Then some obnoxious man, his kid, and his buddy show up. I didn't mean to be such a bitch. But. Whatever.

The man is a jerk, you can tell. He has red hair and muttonchops that are probably meant to be funny. His trunks are ugly forest green and five years old at least. But his kid is worse. This child is the kind that I truly hate. Speech impediment. Loud. Female. An awkward tween with no discipline. Not at all cute. She's got a fat belly, stumpy legs, drooped broad shoulders, and must be totally attention-starved because she stomps right and left and shrieks around her too-young father and his pot-smoking friend. They are men with tribal armband tattoos and budding tans.

They miss her doing a cannonball that splashes water onto my head. I look at my husband, appalled. But. He's not watching. He probably really is asleep.

Safely perhaps, the child flops around in the shallow end of the pool. I do a little breaststroke to get further out into the middle of the pool. I can tolerate a lot. I don't really care what people do. But the wave action she creates is still a problem and I'm here to have fun. I don't want to get too close to those guys she's with. They are lying in the sun at the farthest possible point away from the child. So I'm caught between them while the girl shrieks continually, "Daddy, did you see that?"

"See what? Do it again, Hoss."

Hoss? Now, if I had a child, and I don't—my husband says we don't have the money—and I were a man, which I'm not, and my child were a little girl, which I hope to God I never have, I'm thinking that one of the least endearing terms I could ever use for my daughter would be Hoss. I mean, sure the kid's a little fat, a little boorish, a little—well, yeah, Hoss is apt. But certainly she grew into her expectations.

If I had a daughter, she'd wear dresses every day and have gorgeous long hair that I'd braid across the top of her head or into two matching fishtails. I'd help her with her homework. My husband wouldn't scream profanity at the computer screen in the back bedroom behind a locked door. I wouldn't turn up the volume on the TV. No. My parents would come and visit. They'd stay in the back bedroom. I'd have four pillows for them to choose from and a new, warm blanket that matches the curtains.

I'm not afraid of them or anyone.

The girl in the pool keeps trying to do flips.

I want to be nice. I want to not care that this girl is playing at whatever kind of backflip she hopes that is. Who thinks they can plant a handstand without pointing their toes? She's got one leg bent and both feet angled like an inline Egyptian statue. Lord. I would love to just throw the bratty little ass-child straight up over the blasted fence into the dumpster. Yet I am forced to resort to the much-abused pleasant onlooker who seems to give a shit. Now her dad and his friend aren't watching at all. Dammit. She's made eye contact with me and seems to assume I'm enjoying her show. As if I would ever want to be an audience for her. I'd rather watch my father organize his pressed-penny collection.

Okay. Well. Fine. That was a good one.

She needs to tuck her chin.

Better.

She's just pushing water backwards. Pushing off too hard with her legs and she's not getting the height. Damn, girl. Needs to spring up, then arch her back, then lead with clasped hands.

There. Good. She arched her back enough. Another good one.

But the rest of her tricks have been poorly executed and lacking in grace.

Oh. She definitely got water up her nose with that move.

Plus, she needs to scoot back about five feet to be in a more shallow part of the pool. That water's up to her shoulders. She's fighting all that buoyant resistance. No wonder she's not getting the height. By the time she pushes off, she's already sinking.

Who am I to tell her she's in too deep?

I call out to the girl maybe because of the charge in the sky. "Sweetie!"

The child is defenseless. She looks down at her father. Her father looks at the little girl and then at me. But I have them divided. The little girl treads water and looks at me unresponsive.

The pool is surrounded by crepe myrtle and a mockingbird flicks her tail.

"Sweetie, why don't you just play quietly like all the decent children?"

Finally, she is ready to play elsewhere and stop making all those irritating waves. Good. Her father is up. His friend is glowering but it doesn't matter. She wants to

go home. She wants to watch NASCAR and do the
laundry. She wants a soybean burger and chips.

Resistance dissipates. They leave.

The pool is quiet again and my husband is snoring.

It doesn't matter. I hear the cicadas live their loud
surges after seventeen years. I am watching the side of the
mountain play dress-up with the clouds curling by,
romantic-like. And we are finally alone again at the pool
just like I wanted to be after an electrical storm in the
summer.

JEANIE

Girls with something to prove aren't the best to fall in love with. The best type of girl to fall for is one who has given up altogether—a girl who wants nothing and can't remember if she ever cared anyway. The best type of girl, if you're looking for girls, is a girl who can offer you only herself. You'll know when you meet her. She'll have hollow eyes and never enough to do. But not everyone listens, and sometimes a girl, a stubborn and beautiful girl, gets herself fallen in love with. And then I say, pitying, pompous, loving, kind: *Why don't you ever listen?*

"No. I don't want to, and I won't." Her childhood bedroom door muffled Jeanie's voice.

Her mother held the locked doorknob and leaned heavily against the door, hoping pressure might help her reach her daughter. "But he's come all this way, sweetheart. Don't you want to talk to him? Hear him out?" There was only silence. After a minute her mother heard a page turn. Her daughter was reading and relaxed with no intention of speaking to anyone.

Mrs. B. turned slowly in the hall trying to come up with the right words to offer this young man with his earnest intentions. She didn't want to see his face again. No one had expected him from the way Jeanie made things sound, and yet here he was. He drove over two days to face a family that hated him and a girl who didn't want to open her door. It wasn't right. Mrs. B. pictured the poor boy waiting in the living room. His eyes filled with misunderstanding. His limbs loose and unwanted. His hair meant that he had given up and his smile was too vigorous.

Mrs. B. slipped her hands into the pockets of her apron and leaned back against the hallway wall. Her head knocked a picture frame and she sprang away to prevent it from falling. As it swung on the tiny nail, she looked at the picture. It was from some professional photography studio. Jeanie was two or three in the picture and smiling brightly into the dark hallway across time. Mrs. B. remembered fighting and piling everyone into the car that day. Jeanie had cried all the way to the studio and all the way home, but for a few minutes under the big silver umbrellas of light, which intimidated some of the most brave children, Jeanie basked happily, smiling, and cooing for the camera.

The picture was beginning to turn yellow.

Next to it there was a shot of Jeanie in ballet. She was third from the end in a long row of Saturday morning ballerinas. The other thin little figures stood with their feet together and their arms at their sides. Among them, Jeanie stood resolutely with her arms thrown open and her feet planted wide apart. None of the girls was over six years old, and Jeanie was certainly one of the smaller ones, but somehow the command of her stance filled her smiling mother with courage. It was impossible to know what was going on that moment, whether Jeanie were stretching, behind a step, or just plain ignoring directions, but the picture led one to believe that it was Jeanie, little tiny round-bellied Jeanie, who was bounds ahead of the rest and quickly catching on to the newest motion.

It's probably more foolish for a bunch of little girls from a nowhere town to ever think they could become ballerinas than for them to believe in Santa Claus. But then it's even funnier that mothers and aunts go on encouraging hopes of *Nutcracker* stardom long after Santa Claus and the Tooth Fairy become the silly forgotten nonsense of childhood.

The next picture showed Jeanie with her brothers and sisters and a number of other children at the beach. Her mother remembered the day. Jeanie had organized every child in a two-mile radius into an elaborate game. There were children running along a jetty diligently scraping barnacles and directing the water traffic. There were children pulling beach grass and raking seaweed into enormous piles that other children were building into fortresses. There were children who ran, children who cleared rocks, and children who defended boulders. There were children making piles of clam shells, and mussel shells, and there were children grinding the shells, in exact proportions, into a medicinal slag with rounded stones in the bottoms of six brightly-colored pails. There were children clearing the ravine of the sharpest rocks, and children screaming to one another from king-of-the-mountain vantage points. There were two tiny children looking for live periwinkles for the sake of an activity, and there were some bigger children who stood awkwardly nearby, wishing they were younger so as to be less inhibited and more involved. No one understood the rules. Jeanie was at the center of it all and the children swarmed around her looking for tactical advice, reassurance, a reassessment or clarification of the rules, and guidance. They brought their products for her approval and asked her to mull over this or that strategy and plan.

Most of the children were running nonstop the entire morning but Jeanie sat in her emerald green suit and dark tan on top of a rock dictating the show and making sure to include everyone. When no one needed her she sat looking at the water. Sometimes she looked out at the horizon with conviction. Sometimes she looked down into the shadow of the rock and watched the clinging seaweed thrash in the water. Mrs. B. remembered so much motion from those hours of that day but in the picture Jeanie's little feet were drawn up close to her body. Amid the ocean and the swarm of children she was tiny. Waves crashed all around the huge rock.

To get the best picture, her mother had strolled up, in the way that mothers sometimes do in their broad-brimmed hats, and dropped in to visit the self-appointed queen. When she asked her daughter to explain the game, Mrs. B. remembered Jeanie's saying to her, from behind Mickey Mouse sunglasses, "It's like war, Mommy. No one understands it, so someone just has to pretend so that nobody will be scared. Then everyone will be okay." The game ended late in the day when the troops were exhausted and the queen's throne was overcome by the tide. Even when every child on the beach fights as hard as any full-grown squadron can, they don't defeat the tide.

There were other pictures on the wall but Mrs. B. looked past them and let her eyes rest on another one of Jeanie. She was onstage lighting a candle. It was the honor society induction ceremony her freshman year of high school. No one in the family had heard about the upcoming event. There was no mention of it from Jeanie. Mr. B. had been reading the paper and saw his own daughter's name among those listed to be honored that evening. Confounded, frustrated, confused, he stood up and wandered into the utility room where Mrs. B. was folding towels. He read the article aloud to his wife and then stared at her. It was close to six o'clock. The paper said the ceremony started at seven thirty. They had decided to confront their child with the paper and had gone together down this hall to their daughter's door to ask Jeanie about it. She said that, yes, she was being inducted but that she didn't understand why they had to make a big deal out of it. There was no reason to go. She didn't feel like going. Mr. B. said he didn't really care what she felt like and that it wasn't her decision to make. This had escalated to a loud altercation mainly between Mr. B. and Jeanie.

At seven fifteen the whole family was in the van and they were all in foul moods. There were several complaints of hunger, as dinner was left in cold pots on the stove. B comes early in the alphabet so they hurried. Mrs. B. watched her daughter walk up to the candle and light it without pride. She noticed the smug looks on some of the other students' faces. She witnessed the honor that some students felt, or even the discomfort at being in the midst of such a formal affair. But as all the inductees stood in a row at the end of the ceremony, there was no contempt in Jeanie's face. No hostility. No smug countenance. Her face wasn't blank, really. She just smiled faintly, and waited. Mrs. B. realized that out of all the kids on the stage she only recognized her daughter. None of Jeanie's friends was there with her; such a simple explanation for all her stubborn noise at the house.

Mrs. B. ran her finger along the top of the frame, dusting it.

Another picture on the wall in the hall was of Jeanie and her grandmother. It was the last picture of the two of them before her grandmother had passed away. They were sitting in the garden under a tree with their backs to the camera. The light filtered through the leaves in such a way that only their faces were lit by the sun. Both of them looked at a single pink rose which had struggled its way through the weeds to stand out in the full sun. The profiles of the women were identical. The old lady's lips were parted in explanation of life, and the young woman listened. It was funny enough to smile, even laugh alone in a hallway, because Jeanie never listened to anyone else but her grandmother. And at the funeral Mrs. B. remembered how Jeanie had insisted on speaking. She had also read a Bible verse, which was written on a tiny piece of paper and remained wedged down in the corner of the picture frame. It read: "Hope deferred makes the heart sick; a wish come true is a staff of life. To despise a word of advice is to ask for trouble; mind what you are told, and you will be rewarded. A wise man's teaching is a fountain of life for one who would escape the snares of death."

Mrs. B. laughed at Jeanie's hypocrisy. She had never taken anyone's advice. Not even her grandmother's even if she did listen and learn. She always found a way to prove everyone wrong, or foolish, and most likely had not even thought of the verse since the day her grandmother was buried. But there were the words. Jeanie knew they mattered once. Mrs. B. said, half aloud, "Hope deferred makes the heart sick; like you, my poor child."

She let her eyes pass over Jeanie's high school graduation picture. She glanced at a shot of Jeanie and her father in front of Jeanie's sophomore college dorm that overlooked a lake. Mrs. B. looked for a minute at a picture of all her grown children in front of the Christmas tree. There was another picture just like it from the following year, only Jeanie wasn't there. Mrs. B. reached up and straightened the frame.

She remembered how Jeanie had disappeared two weeks before Christmas. How when she had called her children to breakfast that morning, Jeanie hadn't come down. How they had knocked on her door for over an hour, first annoyed, then anxious, then worried and afraid. Mr. B. and one of their sons had pried the door open with a crowbar, and Mrs. B. half expected to find her daughter dead. It was more of a shock to see the bed neatly made in an empty room. She remembered long searches with the police. She remembered agonizing prayer-filled nights with a God she did not know well enough. She remembered Mr. B. taking them all to the movies to take their minds off things. She remembered finding her youngest son crying in the backyard, and how their oldest daughter did nothing but bake cookies one night. Mrs. B. laughed remembering all the cookies that were made. Every possible kind, six dozen of each. Everyone dealing with the unknown—the excruciating weight of time—in their own way.

Then on Christmas morning, with the bright sun reflecting joy off the snow, there was a phone call. A happy voice filled all the eager receivers in the house with assurance. "Sorry I haven't called. We've been driving forever, and it seems like every gas station's phone is out of order. How stupid is that? Who's we? Oh." She laughed and covered the mouthpiece to scream something at someone nearby. Then back into the phone, "I'm in love. Dad, don't even say it. I know what you'll say, and I say you're wrong. You can fall in love in two weeks, and besides I've known him for almost two months. But the first time we talked was two weeks ago at the bakery. He bought me a jelly doughnut, and I swear it's forever.

"Don't you think it's perfect that I didn't get in touch with you 'til today? No. Well, I think it's perfect. It's like a Christmas present for all of us. So Merry Christmas!" She would have hung up, but someone asked, and she replied, "Oh. Yeah. I'm not really sure. In Arizona somewhere. I'll let you know when I have a real place. Maybe you all can come and visit or something. I can smell the turkey from here, Ma!" But there was no turkey that year. No one had thought of it. They just ate cookies and watched *It's a Wonderful Life*. And they took the picture in front of the tree anyway that year, missing Jeanie.

Mrs. B. took a few more steps toward the living room. She stopped in front of a silly and playful picture of Jeanie and her love. Mrs. B. had never looked at it without smiling, but now she wrinkled her eyebrows and sighed. They must have been camping in the desert. There was a tent and a Coleman stove and a lawn chair. Behind them cacti and sagebrush dotted the landscape all the way to the horizon. There were low mountains on the left side of the picture. It was a joke. Just a snapshot taken by a friend. They had all been drinking. Jeanie was pushing against her love's chest and he, though laughing, had started to fall over. The picture was at least two years old. They had probably wrestled on the ground long after the photographer had forgotten the shot. And Jeanie might only have mailed it for the great smiles on both of their sunlit faces, but in the hall that day, with this boy in her husband's favorite chair, Mrs. B. saw the picture again for the first time. It was devastating to see it so clearly. Her daughter, her mocking, playful, spritely, sarcastic, frivolous, immature, temperamental, evasive, heedless, reckless, unforgiving, so young daughter pushed him away.

Mrs. B. considered turning to the doorway and saying, "Was that verse from Grandma's funeral from Proverbs 13?" But. She didn't ask knowing there'd be no answer.

What must that boy think?

There was a picture that Jeanie had taken of herself. She used a tripod and her father's best camera which had a timer. There was a dark purple thunderhead sky behind her and a rainbow arched itself back over the spruce trees. Jeanie was dressed from head to toe in yellow and stood—arms thrown up—where the rainbow would have touched the ground. A loud statement and strong opinion shouting, "I am a veritable pot of gold, priceless and unattainable." It was a summation. Jeanie with a personality that is impossible to find. Jeanie with a transient confidence that appears comfortable between the harshest, most contrasting conditions, where blazing sun meets the million prisms of an ineffable rain. Jeanie who is only a twist of light. Jeanie, a promise easily broken in a dry Arizona summer.

No one could blame him for his love.

Mrs. B. drew herself up slowly and walked back into the living room. He had gotten up from the chair and was standing in front of the open door near where she had left him. It hadn't been that long. The mat under his feet said, "Welcome Home," and he stared at it.

Neither of them wanted to have to say anything for fear of tears.

But. He was a grown man, not a child, so he said, "Sorry about this, Mrs. B. I thought, well, hell, who knows what I was thinking." He glanced up at her. Her face changed quickly to encourage him with a smile and bright eyes, but he saw her pity first.

She wanted to pull him into some hug that would be enough. But there he was with all the import and fragility of his manhood. *Damn.* She restrained herself, giving whatever support she could by leaving him alone.

He looked down at the shoebox he was holding. There were several small treasures in it. Nothing fancy: a few smooth stones, a picture or two, a blue wax figure of an elephant, a foreign coin, and some other memories no one could possibly share. He laid the box down in the chair he'd gotten up from exhausted from holding such a treasure chest. His hands eased into his pockets and fell asleep at the wrist. He cleared his throat and looked at the clock. He knew that the motion of those hands should mean something, but he didn't see the time. He thought hard. Both of them wished she would just get over it and come out of her room. She didn't. She wouldn't. They both thought she must have fallen asleep by now. They knew her best.

He laughed a little at his own failure and shook his head. With aspiring, raised eyebrows he said, "Well. No sense beating a dead horse, right?" He left before she could see his tears. *Why don't you ever listen?* His car sped away.

Mrs. B. shut the door. Her hand lingered on the doorknob. She looked down at her wedding ring. She moved over to the chair and picked up the box of trinkets. She sat down heavily and picked through them carefully. She lifted out a framed picture of the couple that was wedged in the bottom of the box and made the cardboard sides bow out.

Sighing, she leaned her head back against the chair and held it at arm's length to look at it. They were happy. It was their engagement photo. The one they had taken for the newspaper. The frame was separating at one of the corners. Just a cheap frame from the drug store. Nothing special. Mrs. B. pinched it back together. In a minute she stood up and went to a drawer in the kitchen. She pulled out a hammer and a small nail. She wiped her fingerprints off the glass over the picture with her apron. She walked back to the hallway and found a spot just over the light switch for the picture to hang. She held the tiny frame between her knees and pounded the tiny nail into the wall carefully. She hung the picture and backed away from it. She smiled her own smile as a salute to the two in the picture and turned out the hallway light.

SPARROWS

I wish you had known Marylyn. She tried crying alone on dry nights in the attic. But no one came to ask her why there was all the sobbing and moaning so there was little point in indulging such drama. She forced herself to be sullen for a while, but she kept forgetting and smiling anyway, regardless of having charity teeth.

She wasn't much of a girl. She was the kind of person who was afraid of standing on her own two feet. Not because she didn't trust her feet, but because she knew the world was quicksand. That timidity was her presence. Her hair was a nasty old brown color like shoes that have never been polished and have walked miles and miles in the loose limestone dust alongside the road. Long and straight, like any girl's hair should be, but stringy and hers had a habit of getting tangly. Brushing takes time and patience. No one who's starving knows time and patience.

One of the boys at school used to laugh at the way her shoulders jutted straight out from her neck. He called her Razorback Marylyn saying her spine and shoulder blades reminded him of his daddy's razor. It was just another mean name made from harmless nothing and a bit of prejudice. You know how it is; she was poor. And she knew it. Once you know it you can either give up or move on.

I guess she sustained herself the same way desert plants do. Conservative. Very conservative. Not heedless. She took smiles from strangers in the supermarket as love, and made friends with the people she saw from a distance on a regular basis. Shop clerks, crossing guards, bus drivers—that sort of thing. Just like a desert plant, never expecting too much and adapting, compensating as a result. But not dead. Not at all dead, and in a slow scraggly way moving on in life. No bitterness, no pain, but still dirt poor.

High school was hard on Marylyn. There was no room for her in the well-dressed crowd of whispers and giggles. No one wanted to waste her time on a girl who didn't have anything bad to say about anyone. They called her weak and noncompetitive; said she would not thrive. She had nothing against them.

She spent her lunch hour with her brother and his friends under a sycamore tree near the baseball field. Every day five or six of them sat there in the root dust smoking cigarettes and talking about cars. In the winter, when they couldn't sit down, they'd shield themselves from the wind with that big tree. Their wet feet coiling away from the slushy mud, they still smoked cigarettes and talked about cars. Marylyn didn't smoke. She just sat, or stood depending on the weather, and listened. The boys rarely paid much attention to her. They had too many different cars to dream up and then smash to nothing in their minds using all their reasons for impossibility.

Do you understand the desert? No. I suppose you wouldn't. You water your lawn and let the faucet run while you're brushing your teeth. Well, hold your mouth open for five or ten minutes. Then put a drop of water on your lips and remember that's all you're going to get. It's hard to be poor.

Being alone is virtually impossible. I don't know what drove her. Instinct, I guess. There was nothing to her. She didn't speak, really. She had hardly anyone to care about or who cared about her. That brother was always a little bit loose, if you know what I mean. It's strange really.

But the way I look at it, you can either give up or move on. I guess I already said that. The point is, the only way to give up is to die. Marylyn never died during those high school summers. Others did. Suicide and car wrecks.

But Marylyn wasn't stupid and wasn't a smoker. You might think she would have been. Her mother was. When Marylyn was little her brother used to load cap gun charges down in their mother's cigarettes. The skinny lady would be sitting with one foot pulled up underneath her on the chair in the morning tracing a coffee cup with an absentminded finger and eyeing a sparrow on the sill, all quiet and lonely, then—*bang!* And the barefoot brother would scurry into the room laughing. "Shouldn't smoke, Mommy. It'll kill you." Sometimes the mother would get up and chase him all over, saying, "Let's hope it does, kiddo!" but mostly after those infinitesimal explosions she'd put the cigarette down and forget it. Sometimes the brother cried or he screamed, "I hate you. I hope you do die, Mommy. You never let us do anything fun."

But it wasn't ever a matter of her withholding permission. She didn't ignore her children, or neglect her children, or refuse to answer to her children; there just wasn't any money. So nothing mattered when the sparrow was holding their mother's interest. Her thoughts were simple and repetitive. Such wings, such ugly wings, were all you needed to fly.

Marylyn's mother was ruled by the tiny bird. He was her prince, but she was little if anything to him. Attention and the power of her longing stare were all he needed to go on with his brash, unforgiving tirades. "This and that about the morning dew! And who but the Murphys, with their splintery old feeder, to forget my breakfast! Never had a mind to go anywhere else, but the winds of this place are atrocious! Too much work to leave!" Then Marylyn's mother would bow, nodding an apology.

Flight is the only animate form of perfection. Yet the ugly little sparrow was always bitching about something. The children's mother, those mornings, stared, amazed at such a pompous spectacle. She usually smiled. A vague hesitant smile. It's good to know that humans aren't the only pompous fools.

This was the way things were. There was nothing to be done. He was right. Every morning he would scold her, and then rush off in a huff, while Mother shook her head, missing him. Hoping he would come back if she did the dishes.

Or cleaned up a bit in the living room.

Marylyn—this is back when she was the little razor-backed girl—stood in the doorway out of her mother's view, watching the sparrow too. But she had different thoughts. Come to think of it, those mornings must have been Sunday mornings. There wouldn't have been time to linger any other day. Mothers who work will know. Busy and tired. Always, always, busy and tired. And probably running late. "Ask me again later, dear."

Anyway, the little girl grew up that way. Her yellow-walled room closed in on her, and the mother passed away. Always buying and wrecking cars in his mind, the brother talked on about his own big plans and ended up making do with somebody else's bad habits. He was too used to hand-me-downs, I guess. No big surprises. "Isn't it a shame about the Baxter boy?" "Oh, well, how could you really expect otherwise—what with a mother like that?" There were plenty of looks of concurrence, nods of assent, but then one intrepid white-hair might point out, "But look at his sister. She's doing quite well." "Marylyn?" "Yes. Odd, no doubt. But happy. Doesn't it seem?" And a quick round of nods would hurry across the circle, followed closely by a plate of vanilla sandwich cookies and more coffee.

Inside, alone, Marylyn hated mirrors on account of her teeth. They were mostly straight except one in the front that overlapped the one next to it, and they were all different sizes. Just another gift of charity, I suppose. It seemed as though all the teeth had been taken from other heads and thrown into her smile.

You're not from a small town. It's hard to make you understand. In cities and big places you need names and made-up identities. Names aren't necessary in little places because you know the people and they know everything about who you are. Names are only slipshod approximations. They're cop-outs really. There is more time in small towns. You can watch a person live her whole life in a stereotypic small town. And a name, any one arbitrary word, cannot possibly describe a lifetime like Marylyn's.

Anyway they all watched it happen; she got older and so did her teeth. She bought the pet store and walked to work every morning, with a fresh sweet roll wedged in her jacket pocket.

Some said she knew the baker quite well. It usually wasn't nice when they said this. Others said she was too, well, too something to know quite a bit of anyone. But she walked every morning from the old house on Lincoln Street to her tiny pet shop on the square. She'd get there and look over her shoulder, the folks in the courthouse

said, before she ever fished her key out of a hidden pocket
and began to unlock the rattling door.

Lights on, blinds up. Then—and this is what the
people all loved—she took a careful half-hour setting up a
most elaborate tangle of twigs and vines outside on the
sidewalk. Weather didn't seem to matter. Someone
mentioned to me in passing once that her brother had
built the bizarre sculpture for her out of gnarled branches
from the woods where they used to play. Who knows how
much truth there is in that tidbit? Most people say he
hasn't been much use in years. But Marylyn would set up
those branches, so carefully, and bring out a tiny sparrow,
which no one would think to buy, and place it, so gently,
on a curving twist of a twig.

Customers stopped in through those years of days,
ringing the old cow bell that hung above the door.
Marylyn always said, "Welcome. Glad you stopped in,"
and doled out goldfish like a miner, sold turtles to every
eight-year-old with a jarful of pennies. So much to be
done. There were questions to be answered about this or
that newt. And paperwork on health and cleanliness.
There was money to be counted and saved. Once a pretty
old lady asked if her poodle's pink satin claws could be
manicured. No one ever heard whether Marylyn had done
it; the lady was from out of town. But I believe she

probably painted those claws whatever color the lady wanted. She must have. Why would Marylyn say no? She swept the floor, periodically, and invited summer kids to watch a ferret run through the heating shafts along the floor. At night, when the first streetlights came on, she'd start her closing-up routine, which was rhythmic and tidy and grim.

Even during all this, though, there were long periods of tame times when she would sit at that pet store window, with one foot pulled up underneath her on a stool, looking out, watching her sparrow flit around in its tangle of branches. Such a creature to hop and cock his head and proclaim mightily that there was so little to know which he could not tell you. Marylyn was obliged to listen. Every night he returned to a cage.

FLAG BOX

A violent, vibrant storm rushed in and then vanished leaving a stupid, ripped flag all tangled in our do-it-yourself rose arbor. The one my wife never felt was a good enough incarnation of her dreams. So I took the neighbor's kid, this cute little girl, to use the flag box in front of the post office. It was a week ago. My wife wouldn't have allowed it. But. She was with our three cats at the vet.

I don't think she'll leave me. She's mentioned it twice in the past eight months. But. Hopefully she's not serious. I think she just wants me to get a job. I want to get a job, too. Her staying or leaving really won't change how fast that happens.

I was a chemist. Sort of. Ran gels in a lab until the grant money disappeared. The other two lab techs got spots in the department. They're involved. They do all the stuff you're supposed to do to keep jobs: play the musical chairs, put in five bucks for birthday cakes, talk to the professors and researchers about hockey. I've never been good at that stuff.

There's a thing, you know. Some kind of guy thing. I don't have it. I'm not queer. Been married for almost twelve years. Just never figured it was worth spending a lot of energy pissing all over each other, jockeying for power or whatever like guys are supposed to do. But sometimes it gets me.

I was talking with my sister last night. We were having a theoretical kind of debate. She said she hates being passive, resents it. I don't know what she's talking about. Except that I hate having to be some kind of hero on a stupid old-time white horse. Like it's my responsibility to stop all the robbers on trains. That's not my business. Why don't they just not rob anybody. Problem solved. Plus, no one's ridden horses in a hundred and twenty years. But. People don't care. They still think I'm supposed to save the day. There's no way I'd rescue the pucker-lipped damsel in distress tied to the tracks, punch out some bad guy, run along the roof jumping from one passenger car to the next while a picturesque steam engine blows whistle shrieks into the desert sky.

I don't know. All I know is I saw my neighbor's kid, a little girl about three years old with gold hair that'll no doubt end up losing its curls and shine, outside. She was dancing in a flag. The storm had been terrible. During the worst of it the flag, a pretty large one maybe four-by-six feet, blew off its pole near the cemetery. It got caught in the rose trellis behind my house. When I first saw her running like a bull through a toreador's cape the sky was still purple. July is like that. The sun on one side gleaming. Dark clouds on the opposite horizon grudgingly moving on.

God, she was having fun.

Okay. Now this little girl next door lives under a strange mix of incoherent rules and inefficient supervision. I don't really look out for her. My wife and this little girl's mother are archenemies. I don't remember why. I tried to block it out while it was happening. Conflict's not my thing. But. My wife is basically right. The mom's kind of a nut. So it's not like I'm babysitting. But. I just kind of make sure this little girl's okay out there—not in the street when cars go by if she's running around out front and not falling down into the ravine if she's spinning in circles out back. I don't even think her mom would notice if she ran into the street or fell in the ravine, you know? But I do know that if I instructed her kid even once that woman would come out of nowhere to hunt me down. I can just see her with her big rack flopping everywhere saying I was way out of line and keep my mouth out of her family business. I don't need that shit. I just think it's stupid to let a kid run wild everywhere. Especially when she's in my yard half the time.

So. I stay away from the mother but me and this little girl became some kind of companions after I lost my job. Nothing dirty. I don't have any weird thing for little girls. But. I make sure she doesn't succumb to an accidental death without anyone noticing. It's good. She gives me hope. Well, hope for a second before I remember no one else much cares. So. I've been known to turn the sprinklers on. To leave new beach balls on the lawn. Most days this summer I've watched her race across my yard. And I won't apologize for it.

Anyway a week ago after the storm that wet flag tangled in the trellis surged. And while the wind whipped the red, white, and blue material the little girl raced under it and around the roses, burst straight into the stripes as the wind switched directions and snapped the flag back. She laughed and screamed one or two of those really self-confident little-girl yelps. I had to smile. The sun shone through the colors and highlighted her damp gold hair as the dark clouds receded slowly taking the big winds with them.

Humidity returned. The sky's contrast drained to hazy gray. Her glorious flapping toy dropped to a deadweight curtain, so suddenly tragic—trapped—after just being so brilliant and bold. As if the little girl knew I'd be watching from the window she whirled on me and demanded help with an intense brown-eyed stare.

She's looked at me like that once or twice in the past. I've always stayed inside to avoid that mouth on the woman next door. But last week I felt as sorry for the little girl as she did for that hung-up flag.

I thought of a lawsuit, of the neighbors worrying unnecessarily about an adult man and their little girl, but no matter how whacked-out her mother can be, the moment mattered more.

I ambled across the yard, kneeled down next to that cute little girl, and awaited my instructions.

"We have to help it." She started to cry and hugged me.

Women. Can't hardly please any of them.

For I don't know how many years my wife went on and on about how she wanted a rose trellis. I don't know what kind of grand scale she felt would be worthy.

But she was always pointing out pictures from landscaping books from the library. What was I supposed to do? She's the one who files the tax return. But I did what I could and finally installed one as a surprise on our anniversary.

Shouldn't have bothered. She was immediately disappointed with it. Said the color was wrong. Said it was too rickety. Said the weight of the branches would crush it. Said there was no point growing roses anyway. Threw herself on the bed in a fit of rage because she was too old to start training roses over an arbor in the backyard at this point. But I'd spent a good four hundred dollars on the thing. And paid a guy seventy-five more to dig a few holes, pour some cement, and figure out how to get it propped up. We might not ever live anywhere like that Amalienborg Palace she always talks about going to see but we're not even close to too old for anything. So I started the climbing roses myself.

I wasn't thinking about any of that last week. I was just looking at this little girl with her lip all pouty not knowing how to help the flag. My father's voice became mine. "Well, sweetie, look." I pointed to a corner of the flag which had settled on the wet grass. "Don't let it touch the ground. Flags are never to touch the ground."

She leapt to her duty and stood with her little arms extended far above her head; the flag wrapped wet around them.

"I'll get the ladder, and we'll get it down," I said.

It's not quick, you know. But my roses climbed that trellis just fine. You just tie the branches to it as they grow. That's it. And the color of the thing doesn't matter at all. During the summer you can hardly see an inch of it anymore. And it's not gonna collapse either. Stood up in a storm that tore a flag right off its pole, didn't it?

I came back with the ladder but forgot my gloves. For twenty minutes I wrestled with the rose branches' long, fat thorns. Ensnared material was everywhere because the wind had changed directions so many times. But when I felt like shirking my duty even long enough to just go get the gloves—let alone a big pair of scissors that really would have expedited the process—I'd see that little girl's frame with arms still extended earnestly, with full trust about my words that the flag should never touch the ground. So I worked on. My wet skin burned from the scratches. I looked down at her. "This might take a while. Won't your mother wonder where you are?" She was reverent and stayed silent, her head under the makeshift tent. She reached higher. I saw her little fingers adjust their grip.

I shook my head. "Okay. If you say so."

But damn, I wanted those gloves and that pair of scissors.

Finally I extracted the thing and held it. Together we stood near the trellis and the ladder holding the heavy wet flag off the ground.

She started to get tired, whined just slightly, "What now?"

How should I know? Folding the flag while taps played on a beat-up old trumpet couldn't be arranged quickly enough to give an exhausted three-year-old a ritual tribute.

My arms were poked full of thorn holes and burning. I rubbed my hairy forearm with a couple wide fingers. Whistled low, forcing air through my teeth, buying time.

She kicked at mosquitoes.

I said, "Well, now we take it to the flag box!"

"The flag box?"

"Yeah. They have one in front of the post office. It's where you put old flags."

I put the ladder back and let her pick a special flag container from all the stuff in my shed. We didn't ask for permission to go or really even think of it in the moment. Her mom would have said no for little reason.

I drove carefully but let her ride in the front seat. I think it was a first for her. All these child safety laws with the car seats, you know. But. It was important that she sit right next to me as an equal. The flag lay between us in a wooden apple crate.

She kept one hand on it.

We rode through wet streets in silence. When we got to the post office I showed her the flag box, a converted blue street-side mail drop-box painted red, white, and blue with stars and stripes. I said, "The American Legion puts these boxes out so they can collect and dispose of the flags in an honorable way."

"What's the 'merican Legion?"

I've never been quite sure myself. "They help out with flags and they probably fought in a war."

She listened. And waited, thinking.

I hoped she wouldn't ask me what flags have to do with war. She didn't. She said, "What do they do with the flags?"

I had no idea. They probably burned them in a ceremonious rite. I just knew they handled all the pomp and circumstance required for caretaking flags. "They make sure the stars find eyes to sleep in and the stripes go on end to end from here to California."

She nodded.

I held the flag off the ground while she readied her step. After the apple crate was steady she climbed onto it. I opened the little door and held the back of the flag while she stuffed and shoved and pushed the material into the box.

I tried not to think of mildew. Surely the American Legion folks check the box often. "Not to worry." They seemed the sort.

She kissed the last corner of the flag good-bye, letting her fingers loosen one-by-one. When the last bit slipped away I let the slot's door snap shut.

THE SANDWICH

Stilled isolation and forgotten sock sounds make the harmony of my attempt at beginning.

I don't remember why but I guess a week ago a cop friend called my mother, said he was taking me to a hospital, a psych hospital. Mom came to visit. Felt she had to. Resented it. But. Came nonetheless. It was like usual. Five days to stabilize the meds, to ask all the right questions, to teach me to cope, again, to deal with my mother and the paperwork, and then to set me free as if my mind would allow it.

Mom left yesterday, which is fine.

How do you do your best to sort everything with a glued-back-together-and-held-by-vice-grips mind? You can't ask anyone for help with this part. No one knows what you mean. If they do know, they pretend ignorance.

So just hush and hurry to fracture your constant stream with prism eyes as information comes sideways.

Inanimate things take their toll on me. My socks rest where they were left on an unremembered day. I think about my broken mind and try to let the glue dry. Let it harden while dealing with the coming of a teakettle in the apartment next door. Culling awareness, I put what I hear in different places with their pictures of female members of the family. Or men, sometimes, for the guy sounds. Distant traffic revving at the street light goes into a memory of the accidental night. Gasping hawks get put away with photographs of my father. Inside the socks lay crinkled on the couch and still. Weighing me down with their no-sound way to put them anywhere.

If the floor is, in fact, under the bed, it will not sink, I guess. But who can be sure where the floor ever is?

But if the floor is, in fact, under the bed, then I guess I am pretty hungry. Jell-O would be great. Knox Blox, to be exact. Cut out with nestable cookie cutters of different-sized stars. Slip yellow points into red corners and be good enough, be someone worthy, be happy to put one star inside the other like it shows how to do on the package. But you need vegetable oil that has no flavor to grease the perpendicular-pressure aluminum. I only have sesame oil. And I hate eating art.

So then what? Gravy? I don't know how to make gravy. What'll I do with the lumps? There will be lumps because I am not good enough to make anything come out right. I don't know how to make gravy or anything so they gave me a brochure about self-esteem and said to check a website once a week for coping tips. I can chat in real time with a trained counselor who's twenty-two and makes eight fifty an hour. Sometimes, even so, a yearning rises and grips my center, sending me into a kind of God-lust. Sometimes a yearning comes undone and drifts sideways, changing Mother's hand-me-down thoughts into a kind of almost-wonderland.

Life being half indebted inheritance and half unrealized potential, I am trying to resurface in an unrecognized welcome.

I am awash in similarity. I don't even have what-ifs. But whatever. Instead of getting anywhere with my vision of the meta-almosts I end up with all sorts of not-quite-good-enoughs and probably-could-have-beens and just give up buying anything with built-in obsolescence, like boyfriends and homes, though it seems there is nothing but continuing. No splendor. No deep roots. Simply the day-by-day inebriation of adulthood.

The church tears at the politician who shouts at the people and says, "Hope. Change." Change what?

Hope for whom? Myself with others? My other realms with each other? You have got to be kidding. My rhythm of death-days has become so same, so unending, and I am succumbing to the trance of disbelief that shrouds nations.

But. It's okay. There's a pill for what ails me. Just do the laundry. Clean the bathroom. Hang the towels. Spray 409 on the stove. Water the plants. Go to the gym. Feed yourself. Clothe yourself. Take out the trash. Enjoy things like music, books, TV shows, and beach volleyball. Participate. Learn. Invest. Grow. Plan a trip to meet indigenous peoples in a rain forest and discuss intercultural affairs on an ecotourism adventure that's well-enough controlled to be both liberating and safe. Airplanes are natural. Drive your car. Don't let the gas tank get too low. Pay for things with cash. Live within your means. Hang up the clothes. Mop the floor. Do the dishes. Remember the import of eating a balanced diet, of exercise, of maintaining relationships, of having people over to smell your scented candles, to pet your dogs, to comment on your wall art, to play your piano, to rifle through your medicine cabinet, and to sit back down on your couch pretending nothing ever happened.

The house sits animated but still ready to pounce around me with its penetrating unspoken screams. Ready to emerge as *life moving on.*

Sandwich. Bread. Pepperidge Farm white bread.
Fresh. Mayonnaise. Salt and pepper. Leftover baked
rotisserie chicken breast. Lettuce. Not iceberg but
romaine. Or buttercrunch, I think they call it. Tomato.
No. Tomato on the side with more mayonnaise and salt
and pepper.

The bed is moving. No. The walls are moving. No.
It's the clouds outside the window streaming by. And the
bed is dropping away through the floor I knew didn't
really exist and couldn't.

I have to eat. That's what they say. "You have to
eat." They say if you can feed yourself sufficiently then
you don't have to go to strange places where the doors are
heavier than the walls that ripple, haunted and waterlogged
with similar muzzled lives. So different from seedy hotels.
So same. So eat. I have to eat.

It's not pieces of your mind falling into shattered
disarray again, unsortable. It's low blood sugar.

Sandwich. There must be a way.

Fight. Like Christina in Wyeth's muted grass
world. Make your way to what you want, what you need,
what you have to have. Make a well-deserved sustenance
for yourself—your body and mind.

The store is only three blocks away. You can make
it. You can do this alone. But is there any money? Under

the table in the hall: don't you remember seeing a quarter? Yes. But that's been at least five years ago and it was at home in—well, wherever that was. But the floor was a cheap, lacquered jewelry box from Japan. A tourist trinket and black, almost, under that table. It was dark reddish-fade-to-black hardwood veneer that will never chip off. And the quarter was just there somehow in a beam of sunlight. And I saw it. I didn't pick it up. But I saw it there just like that under the foyer table on the souvenir floor. Still, just like that years ago. But it wouldn't be enough to take to the store today anyway.

Mom said there was money in a drawer. She is always using drawers for things, like money, that shouldn't be hidden, that need to be seen.

But pull yourself toward the creation of a sustaining reality.

Commit to small certainties. The salt will sit on the chicken breast and on the skin from the rotisserie and you will just barely be able to see how you've seasoned it.

I remember sandwiches like that.

I have to eat.

I will make a sandwich like that.

There are three dollars in my coat. I know the money's there. Or at least I hope it is. Hope it hasn't been changed. But it's probably there from the time I bought cigarettes across the street. Good. Yes. Here it is. It's real. I remembered it right and I am holding it with two hands, touching it, checking, counting, assuring myself again, and counting again, but yes, it's here. It's really here. This is one thing that's not an illusion, an expectation, a hope, a change, a delusion, a hallucination, a must-have-remembered-it-wrong embarrassed moment, a confusion, a frustration, a trust, an unknowing, a worry, a panic, a thought-so-but-no. It's real.

So. I won. I'm fine. I remembered it right, which means it's real, I'm fine, and my broken brain didn't process it wrong. Not this time. This time I remembered it right. There was three dollars in my coat pocket. I was right. It's real. It's right here in my hand. It's real. I'm looking at it and it's here. I feel it and it's real.

So the coat and the drawer and as long as the floor is there again we're okay. We're okay and we're not going anywhere without shoes and a hat. Where is the hat? I guess it doesn't matter as long as I have the beach towel memory. The one with the dancing Planters peanut on it from all those lost beach summers. God. When will this glue dry? I need to find my hat. I don't need to remember a twenty-year-old, navy blue, dancing top-hat-and-cane monocled-peanut towel on a clotheslined breeze.

Just focus and find the floor. Test it for rotten spots with your leading toe.

The coat. The drawer. The door. The stairs. And another door to the porch. Fine. I'm okay. I'm okay. Just act normal. No one even knows. No one even knows. No one even knows. No one can see your glazed-cherry-blossom-broken-vase glue drying or all the brain pieces held in place so carefully with direct pressure. Just keep walking. Just be careful. Do everything the right way. Look both ways. Cross the street when other people cross the street. Give up when no one else seems to care. Just relax. Relax. There is nothing emotional or psychological or pathological or anything that needs psychiatric care between here and the grocery store. The sidewalk can't do that. It didn't. So breathe in again and just keep going. Sidewalks don't move. Just keep going. Breathe out again and don't worry. It didn't happen.

It might just be the pills.

Did I take my pills? Did I take them? Or was that this morning? Or yesterday? Or did the pills go through the wall to the teakettle sound where the floor fell down into the sinkhole of a grass world impossible to traverse while dragging two crippled limbs across the field of color that must be carpet hanging like a pet-door trap that keeps out the elements with the help of towels on clotheslines and quarters and breeze under foyer tables on jewelry box floors from five years ago?

Just keep walking.

Don't hold your breath. Don't panic. Don't worry. Don't cry. Just keep walking.

Nothing's happening. Everything's fine. Everything's normal. There's no problem.

And some people do understand. A lot of people have been through this. There were plenty of people in that hospital. This is not just you. You're just the only one in your head. But you're not the only one who this has ever happened to. So. Breathe. Relax. Understand the biochemistry, the physiology, the genetics, the statistics, the probabilities, the diagnoses, the family history, the reasons why.

I remember someone's telling me about a huge revolving door in a supermarket with a tank of fish in the middle. The tank is drained now. Broken. I wonder how they drained it. Hope the fish got out okay.

Don't worry about that. That doesn't matter. It's not related. The money is real and it's related to the sandwich parts you still need.

Grocery store. The fruit is amazing, isn't it? Isn't it? Where does it all come from? All this fruit to all these grocery stores. Can it possibly be used, all this fruit? It can't possibly be consumed. I guess it just goes on sale. Is that it? It's not like the bins of screws at the hardware store. These rot.

Don't waste your time reading little stickers of distant provenance and feeling sorry for soft mangoes.

Mayonnaise. I don't know where it is. Where is it? Bread. And how about pickles? Yes, pickles. There is definitely enough money with the coat and the drawer.

Don't wander. If you can't find the bread, go back to the produce section and start over. Just go up and down all the aisles. Focus. Concentrate. You're looking for bread.

See? There it is. That's where the bread is. That's how you do it. That's how you find things you know must be there.

You're done. Now. Go pay.

Smile at the lady. Just smile at the lady. Pretend. It's all just pretend. Smile again.

Don't look through her. She'll know.

Say, "Thank you. Have a nice day." And say it like no awareness is cascading over you.

Push. Don't panic. Fish don't matter.

The sky seems more.

Back to the house. Back to the house. Back to the house. And breathe. Breathe. If you know it, they know it. So just breathe. Breathe. Carry the bag and breathe.

Up the stairs. There is a lock on the door but the key is here somewhere. I live here so it's okay. I have the key. That's allowed. So go ahead, just ease on in.

Sit.

Okay.

Okay.

Sit. Sandwich.

But the knife. No way. Not today. Just fingers today. Just pull the chicken apart. And use a spoon for the mayonnaise. It's good enough. No knife. Not today. Maybe next time, but not today. Knives are too full of potential. Too easy to take off fingers and toes. Too easy to pull the skin off shins and ankles. Too easy to peel away the eyelids and soft places next to the ears. And so not today. Use the spoon today. Ignore the tremor.

Salt.

Pepper.

And pickles, sitting in the chair by the window.

Finally.

SHOULD: HOW MOMMY ATE HER SOUL

For five years, I've been Mommy. My husband calls me Mommy. My daughter calls me Mommy. My mother and father call me Mommy. I didn't know we wouldn't be able to pay for three kids. But now we're doing what we can for two daughters and a son.

There are more than two thousand hash-marked lines on the beltway between my house and work. I get off at 5:00 a.m. and the only way I get home is by staring at the hash marks off my left front fender. I count them and stay to the right of them.

I don't mind my job. I work nights at a security booth for a gated community. The pay is ridiculously good for the work because the community residents place such a pompous regard on limited access. They value my ability to keep people out. But I don't keep anyone out. The motion-sensored gate does. Not that anyone ever wants to come in who doesn't live there.

My job is easy. There are two hundred gated communities around here. If anyone really wants to get into a gated community to kill people in their sleep, rape the women and children, pillage, steal the pool table imported from Italy, or drive really fast up and down the streets being obnoxious, most likely they will do it somewhere else.

Mostly I get huge tips from high school kids to log times ten minutes before they were supposed to be home. Some nights I'm convinced the parents moved to the gated community just for the logbook. A third party to settle disputes. Often in the early morning there comes a mother in a silk robe driving an SUV. It screeches to a halt behind my booth, and she shuffles up in slippers to scrutinize my entries for the past twelve hours. I don't mind. I like the kids. But kids shouldn't be tipping that kind of money. And no woman who's a mother should be wearing that kind of robe.

I don't tell my husband about my tips. That money goes to the lunchroom at Chateau Neuf with me alone. I thought once about taking Katrina, my oldest girl, for some special mommy time. But I knew her sweet innocence would reveal all to her father. So I let her have special time with him and I keep Chateau Neuf for me.

More often than not after midnight there is no one. And I sleep.

If I can't sleep I look out the glass and stare at the gated community's sewage irrigation fountain. Every community with a covenant has one. A little pond. A pretty fountain. A sign not to swim or fish.

If I am asleep it is the sound of Mr. Hawthorne's running shoes which wakes me. He lives at the back of the community, 10974 Eagle's Wake Trail, Hawthorne, M & N. He runs to the front of the neighborhood and then stretches near the pond. My last duty before I am relieved by the computer is to release Mr. Hawthorne into the world for his run. He is gray-haired and sweet. He always smiles as he goes and shouts, "Thanks, Annie!" with an arm thrown up to the sky.

I counted the hash marks and I'm home. I'm parking my car.

I hear my husband inside the house. He's screaming at my daughter, "Wait for Mommy!" Then he screams toward me, "Hurry up, Mommy!"

I'm sitting in the garage, in my car. I can hear my husband calling. His voice holds so much. He thinks he'll be late. He's convinced that it's my fault. He was up all night with one of the kids or the baby. If I was any kind of mother I would have been the one there for them. After all they were calling for me, not him. He can't find the shoes he wants to wear. He forgot to pick up the dry cleaning so he doesn't have the shirt he wants. If I was any kind of wife I would be the one ironing. There's no food because no one went shopping this weekend because we had to go to that stupid christening/wedding/high school graduation party/fiftieth anniversary celebration/work picnic/Christmas gala and why should I miss the game just to get groceries?

His calling me says all of this and more. It doesn't always say *I missed you, I still love you, I need you to work so we can pay for the tree house that we bought on credit and then destroyed in the assembly process.* And it never says *Welcome home, dear. Did you have a good day at work?*

For some reason I go in. I stare at the fruit bowl during our changing of the guard. He rushes past in a swirl of resentment, late for work.

Hours later he is back. I hear myself say, "Welcome home, dear. Did you have a good day at work?"

"You would never believe these assholes." His voice trails off as he walks down the hall. He keeps talking for two hours from this point. Every day.

It's not that I don't care about his work. I guess I do. I certainly should.

At the first hour into his monologue there always comes a single line. It doesn't vary much from this: "If I got a decent night's sleep once in a while I could handle it."

We settle onto the couch. We turn on the TV.

What my husband doesn't realize is that for all he knows I don't sleep. He has never seen me at work. He must assume I am working. And yet he never sees me sleep at home. So the gall of him; even uttering this line in my presence is unbearable. I hear myself say, "I suppose so, honey."

And then once he passes out, I leave for work. I don't count the hash marks. When I drive toward work I just feel them pulling me in, closer, closer, closer, to that little hut.

I read a note that my boss has left for me in an envelope. It says that I should not park my car in the driveway of the sales model. Someone has likely complained. Though why I cannot imagine. My car is parked there from ten thirty at night until five in the morning. Who could possibly care whether there is a car parked at the model during that time period?

I'm not sure whether I should move my car.

Where should I park?

I decide to leave it for tonight and will call my boss tomorrow to find out where I should park.

I clock in and start my shift.

Hours do not help.

What helps are seconds.

I know that time is passing if I think about the seconds.

I'm counting them when I hear the sound of familiar footsteps.

There is one woman who comes to my booth almost every night. She wears her robe and slippers. She comes with a thermos and a radio and a deck of cards. Her husband is having an affair and her children never obey their curfew. She sits with me in my booth and we have a great time. She watches others pull through the gate. She writes down the time and then we play cards until she passes out in a heap on the cement floor. She has an air mattress that she stows in my booth cubby. Rarely does she bother to inflate it. When she does it fills up the entire booth. She sits on it like a chair with part on the floor and part going up the wall where the door is. It is hysterical. She always brings her stainless steel thermos. Sometimes she just brings coffee but more often it is filled with white

Godiva liqueur, Kahlua, and three cups of vodka over ice. She calls her thermos the Stealth Bomber.

We laugh a lot about the thermos.

I have never known her name. Her address is 12488 Peregrine Falcon Lane. Her husband is William F. Fessner. She told me once that she kept her maiden name. But she never told me what it was. Interesting. I worry sometimes that I will read in the paper that a certain woman has committed suicide. It will be her and I will never know from her name.

But we both like the brilliant red leaves on the Virginia creeper around the little gatehouse. We love how unbelievably bright red they are before that first frost, that driving October rain, that mess they become in the street once they fall away.

MI FANTASMA QUERIDA

With clenched pain in my chest and numbness radiating down my left arm I woke in my bed an hour ago and thought, "So it will be a heart attack." If the morning sun were to rise over any other patch of water, then I would be there. But it does not. It rises here and rears back ready for the day. It is an uncommon thing. Swollen light waits, dormant, just below the surface. But it's my time. I'm eighty-seven. The sun leans into her work. She does not relent and with a submitting grace steps forth into the deepest part of a purple sky. Why call an ambulance or go to any hospital? The sun, like a queen-child of kings and godless men alike, moves across a well-worn sky-path with confidence. When the night takes her, there is rapture.

I wanted to call my daughter. But what kind of call would that be? Plus, I didn't want to wake her. I'm in New Jersey and she's in Denver. There's a time difference and she only gets a few hours of sleep as it is because of the baby. So when the pain eased enough to sit up, pull on a shirt, and stand, I just muttered a prayer to St. Teresa of Avila for my daughter. *Nada te turbe. Nada te espante. Todo se pasa. Dios no se muda. La paciencia todo lo alcanza.* My mother said that prayer so often to me as a child. And she told me stories from Saint Teresa's *Interior Castle.* Stories I told my daughter. *Quien a Dios tiene nada le falta. Solo Dios basta.* So that done now I just move from my bed, grab the door to support my weight, ease myself through three rooms and out onto my sagging little porch.

In agony I bend over and pick up my little fishing pot with the knife, a couple hooks, some drop weights, and a spool of line. I bang the pot between my rocking chair and the window so my ghost will sense it is time to go fishing. She is deaf but senses something. The vibrations maybe? My scent? I don't know. But I want her with me so we can go down to the beach, down to my little rowboat, to face what is meant for me.

Sabby, this large white dog, bursts through the underbrush between the houses before I even call her twice. She is always excited to go fishing with me. I doubt

I called her loud enough. I'm sure she just heard the screen door scrape the sagging porch roof and came bounding to me because of that. But she sees me, sits, tilts her head, then seems to know before I can tell her anything about what will happen. I stand sweating on the porch with the huge dog still staring at me.

The neighbor lady used to get mad that I take her dog fishing. She didn't think a purebred show dog should be out on the water in some old man's boat, especially not some old brown man's boat. But the dog always wanted to go with me. I suppose because we're both Argentinian. After a few months the owner eased up, said Sabby's fishing with me would be fine as long as I never took her out past the sandbar, in case she ever needed to swim back. My neighbor is a nervous woman and seemed to want me to know how precious a thing I carried. So she stood there next to me on the beach one morning— looking at the ocean, not me—and explained all the trouble of getting this special dog. On the papers, her name is Fantasma de la Sabiduría, the dam was Sombra de una Duda, the sire was Triturador de la Nube. My busy self-important neighbor doesn't know I call her Sabby. It is fitting. But often I call her Mi Fantasma Querida, my beloved ghost. I wrote a poem for her.

My beloved ghost, whose yesterdays are the eyes of God.

Usually I say it in Spanish. It sounds better.

Sabby does not have her ears clipped but severity remains in the readied shoulders and down deep between her eyes.

The pain comes back.

I can barely stand and think of just sitting for a moment in the chair. I know I'll never get up, though. So I stand, lean against the wall of my little cottage until the big, white dog stands up and comes toward me. Months ago I trained her to carry my fishing pot in her mouth by its handle. So she grabs it from me. Her profound patience stills my mind. She never once looks away from my eyes.

When the pain eases again we move to the stairs and take them one by one together. She lets me lean on her shoulders as we cross the beach to the boat and thank God for the high tide. I only have to push the boat a few feet to get it into the water. But. I can't lift the anchor from the sand. I consider for a moment and then decide. I cut the anchor rope with my fishing knife. It is still a lot of exertion but not as much as lifting the deadweight of that anchor in the sand.

I push the boat off and climb in. Sabby jumps from the beach into the boat and sits patiently on the floorboards as I fit the oars into the oarlocks. The sounds are familiar to me but she hears nothing.

I used to be a fisherman. But I've been retired long enough that the longing for the smell of diesel fumes over saltwater is gone. I don't miss the plastic crates of fish submerged in the holding tank. Nothing as recent as those years matters. What I remember is standing on the rocks near my childhood home fishing with my dad and brother.

My brother died in 1973 right before my father forced me to come to the States. My brother had gotten himself involved in all that political tumult. There was a mob of protesters moving down a side street and he ended up crushed between a trash barrel and a wall. I never got all riled up like he used to, never got involved in the insurrection, but my dad still didn't think it was safe for me there at home. Though why he thought I'd be better off living in his aunt's basement in New Jersey I have no idea.

But. He was elderly then himself. Wanted me to get out of La Boca.

I miss those black rocks where waves slide back down into the sea like a hundred snakes. That's where I stood and fished for corvina with my brother and dad. And I remember my mother taking both of us, my brother and me, on the bus thirty kilometers inland along the Rio Negro to Viedma for my first communion. I'd never seen anything so beautiful as the Cathedral of Our Lady of Mercy.

This is pain like I have not known. But I'll be with my mother, my brother, and my dad soon. In no time.

Heather grows along the bulkhead. Someone— Nuestra Senora de la Merced, maybe, but definitely someone unknown to any of us along this stretch of beach—planted it here during the 1940s and it abounds in the spray of the surf. Like the ruff of a little boy's hair the heather swirls and tosses in the wind that comes down through two tall rocks at the horizon. That whipping breeze hugs the cliffs and the sandy beach. And we smell the seasons before their time.

I only have a rowboat now. *The Reprieve*, I call it. There was once a fishing boat and then a charter fishing boat, but they are both gone. One was stripped down and rebuilt for a radio station to broadcast advertisements to the throngs along the bayside beaches. The other I burned here near the heather. But this little dory does just fine.

The rowing will be difficult for me. Sabby notices how slowly we drift through the water. Her satiny white body is muscle-bound, alert, but she is in no rush. She is as old as I am. And there is no hurry left in either of us.

She lies down, leans against the side of the boat, and shuts her eyes.

For a moment we rest on a glassy impossibility. The air is still. The water is flat except at the very edge where imperceptible waves give in, repeating a hushed lullaby for the slumbering sea. The birds on the cliff are done with their dawn songs. The gulls preen themselves on the jetty and stand looking to the north. There are no other boats this morning. Once there were many fishermen but now the beach is for weekends, not work. The water drips from my oar in three places. The sea receives the drops in a dignified series of ripples. I see the sand and rocks of the beach beneath us steeped a yellow-green at high tide.

We move out in rhythmic thrusts. My companion is awakened after her short drowse on the cross thwart. She climbs over my seat. Rising up, she places her front paws on the transom and looks back at the shore as I row out onto the water.

I like to get out past the sandbar, even if my beloved ghost's owner doesn't like it. Fish in the shallows don't bite for me, it seems. The fish are in colder water beyond the sandbar so we're three-quarters of a mile offshore and, if I had it, it'd be time to put the anchor down.

It takes me so long to lift the oars out of the oarlocks and stow those smooth pieces of wood. But I manage it the way I like. I slide them back behind me, get the handles crossed down under the back seat and the blades vertical along the gunnels.

A cormorant eases by and sits on a boulder which rises out of the water to the east. Our eyes follow its journey, but the bird is nothing uncommon. We always see cormorants when we're fishing in the morning.

If I am fishing, sometimes my past comes to me. It comes and strokes my hair like a mother. And I rest wearily against it as events occur again. I remember others laughing and my jokes that would last for days. I remember the ocean water in all her costumes and moods. I remember the oceangoing charters and an Atlantic full of fish. Now that is all so close to nothing. The fishing line is wrapped a hundred times around a piece of driftwood. I can barely tie a hook to the line and have nothing for bait but I am fishing still. I drop the hook easily over the side of the boat. It is held plumb with a tiny lead weight.

The sky is colored an early-morning steel. And the blue-gray waters meet it in every direction. "Mi fantasma querida. My beloved ghost." She comes closer and I stroke her strong back, reciting my poem for her:

Mi querida fantasma, ayer es los

ojos de Dios. Mi querida fantasma, manana se entiende
para ser

dejada excesiva y a nada más.

Mi querida fantasma, convengo

con el viento cuando dice, "Cambio."

Y el cambio siguiente, el viento me

dice que, se duren.

She lies down with her paws outstretched. Her head rests next to me on the wooden seat. And she says nothing. The line is heavy with a catch. But it is likely a sand shark, so heavy in these small waters. I release the driftwood spool into the water and forget fishing. I hold the edge of the seat and lean back under the morning sky, to see its everything once more so fully, and feel the waves rocking the small boat, pushing us. We are tethered to the water by no anchor rope. And the waves push us east well beyond what would have been its limit.

This pain comes and goes. But it is too much. I want to lie down now.

The dog helps me get onto the floor of the boat. I am soaked by the water in the hull, but it is a familiar thing, and I cannot doubt its pleasure.

"Mi fantasma querida, usted debe saber, yo está muriendo."

Her eyes see into me and say, "Shhhhh. It will be okay."

I wonder. "Le creo. ¿Pero mi fantasma querida, dónde voy a ir? ¿Cómo yo deje para ir?"

She sits up and looks straight into the splitting place between the ocean and the sky. It seems, with the colors of the dawn, that no such place exists. But she looks straight into it and does not balk. She is saying, "That is where you are going. And do not be afraid."

I hold her satin body next to mine and wonder who will find us. An early-morning beach walker, maybe. A man drinking coffee up on the cliffs. They will say, *Why is that old man's boat drifting away past the sandbar? Why is the dog there? Where is the man? What a strange picture postcard for our memories.* And I will be lying here on the floor of the boat where no one will be able to see me. And it will be a somber picture from the beach—boat, three-quarters of a mile offshore, with a huge white dog wearing its loyalty and pride. And so it will be against a steely ocean that they will find me. And so it will be with a neighbor's dog that they will find me in the bottom of *The Reprieve*.

Mi Fantasma Querida looks into the impossibility. She looks straight into the invisible morning horizon and escorts me. The boat drifts further, my last grip around her loosens, but she does not quiver.

HOLSTERS IN THE GUEST ROOM

Roni'd been cleaning, breastfeeding her son, and wiping dog slobber off the floor for the better part of the day. When her son vomited breast milk all over both himself and her, she was already running late to pick up her husband's college friend from the South Shore. Roni changed the baby's clothes, put him in his swing, jumped in and out of the shower for thirty seconds, threw on her husband's old FBI SWAT training tee shirt, put her five-month-old son into his carrier, and grabbed her keys. "Jesus Christ," she said under her breath but didn't stumble on the guitar that her dog must have knocked down again with his big wagging tail.

She pulled her wet hair up, picked up her son in his bulky, crash-test-rated car seat, dragged it through three rooms, shoved her feet into some old wedge flip-flops, and rushed through the laundry room toward the garage.

She tried to think about what she'd say to Brandon's friend. She couldn't remember if this was the guy that ended up going to the police academy at the same time as Brandon or if this guy worked with her husband at the stromboli place for five years. She should know. So she couldn't ask. Maybe she could ask him whether he had any good stories on Brandon from when they first met. She definitely wanted to clarify which guy this was before she got back to the house to make their dinner.

Either way she was about to miss his train if she didn't hurry. Hopefully she could catch mostly green lights on the way there and be at the front of the line of cars picking up commuters. She hurried to the garage steps as best she could while lugging the awkward baby carrier because she hated being in the back of that Kiss & Ride line more than she hated being in a rush to leave the house. But at the foot of the garage stairs she just stopped.

Her navy sedan was backlit with blinding light off the cement. The garage door gaped.

She gripped the handle of the baby carrier but didn't look down at her son. All the motion and momentum that had gathered in the past ten minutes dissipated to nothing. It wasn't even worth hesitating. She took the first step and stood on the second step of the garage stairs overwhelmed by both knowledge and disbelief. It took brute force to move up one more step and stand immobilized on the third shocked but not surprised. She stared into the backseat of her car.

She didn't hope. She didn't pray. She just said to herself, "I really don't need this right now." She climbed the last step and stood on the garage floor. Her son kicked his feet in the carrier. She shifted the thing from one side of her body to the other.

Brandon's friend's train was due to arrive in ten minutes. But it didn't matter. What choice did she have? She had to deal with this bullshit again. She set her son's carrier down on top of a fifty-pound bucket of dog food and sent a text to her mom: *What happened?*

Then she walked around to the other side of the car to be sure.

Her husband's motorcycle lay tipped over on the pile of recycling.

Yep.

God damn it.

The driver's side passenger door was standing wide open and her father lay passed out in the backseat.

Roni felt nothing. She just wanted her dad out of her car. She wanted him not there at all. Inert like the mountain bikes, the garden hose, the lawn seed spreader, the broken fire pit, the black shelving, the bag of bulb fertilizer, the snow shovel, the weed whacker, the new wagon, and the crib box, she just blinked. She didn't cry. She didn't scream. She didn't throw anything. She didn't abandon her son. She didn't kick the aging, tyrannic bastard.

She said, "Dad. Wake up. Get out of my car. I need to go. I need to be somewhere."

He didn't move.

She pushed her dad's knee gently but firmly by shutting the car door against his shins. He didn't notice. She picked up each of his legs and let them drop. They were deadweight. She poked him in the chest. He was nearly lifeless—didn't respond to any stimulus. She tried to drag him out of the car but he was too big. She had trouble enough lugging her son around. There was no way she could move her father. It was an exercise in futility to even push isometrically against the accumulated weight, resistance, and friction of their intolerant years. She tried to shove her dad into the car but his clothes against the upholstery of her car seat created too much drag for her to overcome.

Her son started to cry.

She looked over at him, balanced there in a plastic safety device on the dog food. What was she even trying to protect him from? She hadn't noticed any of the dog food scattered across the concrete floor, or that raccoons had likely been in her garage. Her recycling was chewed up and torn. There were scat pellets. So then she did feel something. Not disappointment, rage, or aggression having anything to do with her father's being so exhaustingly who he was. No. She was infuriated that the garage door had been open all night and that wild animals got into her dog's food.

She walked around the car to the big bucket of dog food and started rocking her son. He fell asleep fairly easily. She moved him off the dog food container and put him in the middle of the hood of her car. She got a blue-handled broom and dustpan to clean up what she could. She sprayed urine remover in all the places she found scat.

Her mother texted her back about what had happened with her father last night.

Roni read her mother's explanation but did not respond. Instead, she texted her husband to say that she was going to miss his friend's train. She gave no explanation to her husband, just told him to text his friend and let him know.

Her husband was livid and responded right away. He said, no, he wasn't going to text his friend, that she just needed to go and pick him up, that there was no reason for her to be late, she was just sitting around all day, and that it's not like his friend can just call a taxi—it'd cost a fortune if any ghetto cab even did show up. Her husband's follow-up text said that he never should have given her any responsibility and that he knew she didn't like his even having friends but that she had no right to leave the poor guy hanging.

She did not cry. She did not call her husband at work to scream at him about her father's lying passed out drunk in the backseat of her car. She did not throw her phone down and stamp on it. She did not call her friend to get the name of that divorce lawyer.

She absorbed what she could and did nothing.

After twenty-nine years of listening to all her mother's excuses she was not about to explain anything about this to her husband. She was too sick of all the reasons why. She did not respond to her husband at all. She just looked at her son on the hood of the car to be sure he'd be okay there for another minute and disappeared into the house. She returned with a plastic cup of water, walked around to the rear passenger door, and threw the water in her father's face.

He blinked. He spit. She was patient and maybe a little afraid when she told her dad to just pull his feet into the car because they had to go to the train station. He reluctantly did it.

Roni took her son off the hood of the car and put his car seat into the carrier base in the backseat next to her father. She didn't want her son so close to her father right at that moment but she had no other choice. She was just glad that her child was encased in plastic, that her father was not quite conscious, and that she'd be picking up her husband's friend in a minute. She might not remember exactly how he and Brandon met but she knew he was a big guy trained for mortal combat.

Knowing that helped her breathe.

She got into the driver's seat and adjusted her mirrors. Her father only momentarily met her gaze in the rearview mirror before he tilted his head back and put his hands on his forehead.

Roni said nothing.

She put the key in the ignition and turned it.

Nothing happened.

The car wouldn't start: the battery had run down with the dome light shining all night.

She texted her mom to ask if she could go get her husband's friend at the train station. Her mom immediately responded to say she couldn't because she was almost at work already and plus she didn't understand why her daughter was always so unfeeling about everything that happened and never cared what her mother was going through. Roni should really not give her any more stress right when she was so emotional after the events of the previous evening, and even if she might have maybe considered doing a favor for Roni, even if she were perhaps available for another twenty minutes, she wouldn't do anything right then because she was so mad at Roni for not even responding to her explanation in the other text.

Roni deleted the text message from her mother and got her son and his carrier out of the car. She left her dad rolling around in the backseat and walked to the house next door. She wished she had grabbed the diaper bag or at least a blanket. She wanted to be more prepared. But it was too late. She rang the doorbell.

Her neighbor answered. Roni extended her son's carrier and said, "Can I borrow your car for a half-hour? I'll fill up your tank." Her neighbor didn't say a word. She reached for the baby carrier, dug into her pocket, and handed Roni the keys.

SMALL TOWN

Suicide's unthinkable but around six thirty on a winter night in 1994 the redheaded woman stood against a low building covered with dingy white siding. She had on the suit she'd worn to a job interview she'd never gotten a call back about and smoked her cigarette behind a holly bush because she didn't want to be hit by the door that swung open periodically. Her discount heels sank down into the slushy bark mulch. Her head tilted back against a black oval sign that read, "Devalle Funeral Home" in tasteful gold script. The sign was lit by a solar-powered fluorescent landscaping light full of dead bugs from the summer.

The winter sun must not have fully charged the power cell during the day so its flickering bluish light illuminated her hair. She was tired but not too tired to notice the sign behind her head, to remember the building's purpose, and to realize people were staring at her. She took two steps forward. Her shadow grew tall and black against the siding. She was conscious of the eyes upon her but not of the enormous shadow shifting and flickering behind her. The mourners turned away, afraid of the towering, swaying silhouette. The redhead couldn't understand why they refused to acknowledge her. She knew every one of them. So she summoned a defensive pride and smiled at each of the people she thought judged her for smoking, or for standing in the bushes, or for sinking into the mulch, or for leaning her head against the fancy sign, or for not going inside right away to pay her respects, or whatever their reasons were. She had no reason to be guilty. She was waiting for her friend. So with spiteful clenched lips she nodded to those who refused to look at her as if to say, "And what makes my life your business?"

It's hard to feel absolutely comfortable in a small town.

There's not a large degree of discomfort. After living there for a lifetime a person might not notice any uneasy feeling at all but there is a small amount of tension, like the constant hum in an electric wire or the inescapable buzzing of a ceiling fan that needs repair. It's a uniform, predictable, smooth tension. It must come from the nature of the people. Different figures carved from the same stone, all trying to discern themselves from each other, like kitchen magnets that won't stick together.

And the red-haired woman felt that tension acutely while she waited for her friend. Her hands were bony and freezing in the wind, and even though her heels sank into the muck that February had made of the summer landscaping she didn't want to wait on the sidewalk amidst the influx of mourners. People wearing dark coats passed her. Each one went ahead, stamped his or her feet on the Astroturf step, and held the glass door for the next person.

She was unconscious of the shadow, but it kept happening that as the mourners approached the funeral home they saw the enigmatic figure as a presence to be reckoned with. They passed her without looking. They gripped their children's shoulders. Unconsciously the men placed themselves between her and their loved ones: protective, afraid. The shadow stretched up the building and wrapped itself around the gutter. It was a reminder of the size of death and the reason they had come. They bowed their heads in reverence for the unknown. Her shadow swayed back and forth in the cold, smoking and waiting for a friend. To the passersby the motion signified an impatience with life and a cool expectation of their similar fate. Consciousness is exhausted by February. They did not think all of these things, but the woman's tracing brought tears to their eyes as they passed. The redheaded woman stood aloof, smoking her cigarette, and waiting for someone of these supposed friends to at least say hello. Her "Hello, Irene," crashed useless against the sidewalk.

An old red Chevy truck approached. Graceful curves of slush sprayed out from the wheels, and halfhearted flurries dove past the headlights. The truck came to a treacherous stop and leaned against the curb, exhausted. The passenger asked the driver, probably again, to escort her in. He reached across her and pushed the door open. It scraped the curb, sticking in the grassy mud. A fat woman backed out of the truck and stood on the curb. With her weight removed, the door rose from the mud. She still spoke to the driver. He nodded. The fat woman shut the door and checked her makeup in the side mirror before the old truck pulled away. She smacked the fender in disgust. She hadn't finished primping before her husband drove off. But. He didn't stop. She made her way carefully along the curb to the sidewalk.

The red-haired woman moved away from her post between the landscaping light and the sign it lit. The shadow shrank down the wall and disappeared. People on the sidewalk smiled and nodded as she passed them with her arms crossed tightly over her chest. She watched the fat lady's balancing act with interest. She was nominally excited for the fat woman when she successfully made it to the sidewalk without falling into the slush-filled gutter or toppling over into the soggy grass. The fat woman's brand-new high heels made the event preposterous. Dropping her cigarette, the red-haired woman, who was much skinnier than her friend, clapped sarcastically, despite the others. The fat lady giggled but silenced herself quickly. Laughter was not appropriate with a dead young man inside.

The redhead greeted the fat woman's smile with an eager wave, justifying her wait to whoever was around. The two women fell in line with the other mourners on the sidewalk, stepped onto the Astroturf together, smiled at the man who held the door for them as he went past and out into the night with hollow, dutiful, thank-God-that's-over eyes.

They had to go through with it now.

The fat woman struggled out of her coat. She stuffed her hat down one of the bulky sleeves and her scarf down the other. She laid the coat over her left arm, began diligently picking lint off her blouse, and signed the guest book.

While her friend pondered over what to write as a condolence, the redheaded woman smoothed her hair and pulled at her skirt, fighting its static cling. She looked around. Flowers were balanced precariously on mismatched antique end tables. Men in dark blue or gray suits were huddled together around the edges of the room missing their cocktails. Children—looking sad since they knew Tuesday is never supposed to wear Sunday's clothes—sat waiting, draping themselves without hope of comfort on satin-striped divans in the foyer or on wooden folding chairs that defined the expectation to stay for a while in the spacious front room. Though the husbands and children were removed and recalcitrant the mothers resolved to stand in line to be received and pay their last respects.

As each woman approached the casket, she snapped her fingers in the direction of the perimeter of men, stared at the number of bored, quietly-swarming children, and hissed specific names, summoning the rest of her entourage. One after another each matron made it to the front of the line, the husband came over, sheepish with guilt. The children's porcelain faces betrayed no pain of awareness or understanding even as their mother's fingernails dug into their sweet, awkwardly well-dressed shoulders. Each woman guarded her own. She instilled undeserved strength into her little clan. Keeping herself between them and the casket, they faced death together. This mother was strong. She looked the grieving mother in the eyes as if to say, "I'll shit if this ever happens to me. And if any one of these ungrateful family fools of mine do to me what's been done to you, I swear to God, I'll kill them all." But that went without saying as the graceful, Christian sympathies rolled out of well-intentioned mouths.

The red-haired woman and the fat woman didn't have anyone to summon other than each other. So they just stood shoulder-to-shoulder with their hands clasped in front of them, watching women they knew at the front of the line. The aisle carpet had been worn through by years of mourners' shuffling shoes. In the carpet underneath the wooden folding chairs, pink ribbon reins that spanned a navy background held gaudy textile bouquets together and tight. The red-haired woman tried to decide whether it was possible to have that kind of carpet in a home. She couldn't. She just knew she'd never have it at her house. The fat woman slightly behind her leaned forward and whispered, "I still can't believe he did it."

The red-haired woman pulled the shoulder strap of her purse closer to her neck. In the same motion, a furtive finger grabbed her sneaking bra strap and cinched it back into position. Knowing you are not supposed to allude to bra straps with such gestures, she leaned into the ear of the fat woman. "It's unreal. You wouldn't expect it out of such a sweet kid."

"I don't understand. My kids always thought he was so great."

"He was. Because look at his mother. Marion is just wonderful, isn't she? Look at her with that girlfriend of his. She hasn't let her hand go for fifteen minutes."

"Well, you know, that was his ex-girlfriend. They had broke up about six months back."

"Really? I guess I didn't know. Whenever my kids graduated I stopped getting most of the high school gossip." She tossed her head back to force a bothersome strand of hair to fall out of her eyes. She wrinkled her nose to squint toward the girl. She needed glasses but looked at Marion and the ex-girlfriend. "Well, then that's maybe another reason he pulled this stunt."

"I don't know that you could call something so drastic a stunt. He just needed some kind of help, I suppose. Don't you think? I don't know, really. My boys always said he was an odd sort. They never bothered him much, you know. Nothing wrong with him or nothing— just a weird kid."

"He wasn't weird. How was he weird? He was a sweet boy. And a point guard."

The skinny woman was looking at an elderly couple across the room. She produced a bright smile for them, and then saw them turn to discuss her identity under a green straw hat and with the support of an old cane. She knew what they were saying: pregnant in high school, abused, divorced. She'd heard it all before. Felt like carrying her college diploma around with her half the time. Wanted to see that woman even try to work two jobs, get her kids from daycare, and still cook dinner while she finished her degree. But. It didn't matter. She knew what they were saying: *Now which one is that? Is that Irene's daughter or the one who ended up taking everybody's head off at the ecumenical bake sale two years ago?* Whispers, nods, and shaking heads got tossed back and forth between the old couple. One of his arthritic fingers jumped at the moment of enlightenment, and the green hat rose and fell in agreement. With a curt nod to the old couple, the redhead turned back to the fat woman.

"He was on Jim's Little League team back ten years or so ago. All the pictures he's in the middle of the back row tall as can be and showing off that big grin he had. His mother loved that sweet smile."

"Did he smoke? I thought I saw him smoking over by the grocery a few times. Maybe that was something."

"I don't think so. Do you, really? No. Well, they all smoke." She smoked two packs a day. "Even my boys once in a while. But I'll tell you, when my brother-in-law came off with that cancer, I didn't smell it on my sister or him much anymore."

"Don't you just love it when they think you don't know?" The fat woman leaned in with satisfaction, patting the redhead's freckled forearm. She withdrew her hand modestly, and tried to pull her blazer close around her large midriff. She went on. "I used to go up to my oldest son when he was first in high school and give him a big hug or ask to make him a big dinner when I just knew they'd been drinking beer up at Cawlyer's farm. That poor boy would roll his head back, hold his breath, whatever, just trying not to say anything right into my nose. And he would just reek of alcohol. Frank and I would go to bed and just laugh." She chuckled mostly over the mention of her bed in a funeral parlor.

The red-haired woman thought about the fat woman in bed with the skinny pickup truck driver who had dropped her off. They were an odd couple. Always had been. The red-haired woman tried not to cringe. She sucked in her cheeks and raised her eyebrows. Her response was calculated, an admonishment not at all her own, but one that showed her effort to remain neutral. "Those boys can be so cruel to each other with that beer."

The fat woman regained her composure with a cleansing sniff, giving her full attention to the small talk. She sensed condescension and did not appreciate it. "Oh. Well, my boys never did any of that. But they like to have a good time, just like anyone."

"I've never been much of a drinker. My father was an alcoholic. You knew that."

"No. Now I didn't know that."

The women took several steps forward. The people behind them moved in closer. The fat woman was uncomfortable and someone stepped on the back of the redhead's shoe. Both women turned half-defensively, then recognizing a local pastor and his wife they nodded, graciously forgiving the infringement, probably hoping he would return the favor.

He didn't.

The redhead went back to her story. "He was. It was awful. I don't remember too much about it, but he used to beat up my brothers pretty bad. My oldest sister says that he used to hit my mother, but I don't believe he would do any of that."

"Frank hit me once."

The redheaded woman had never heard that. She rolled her wedding ring around her finger with her right hand. She looked down at it. Remembering where her husband had bought it, she suddenly let it go. "Well." She didn't say it: Everybody gets hit once.

At least.

The fat woman tried again. "Were you the youngest then?"

"Well, close. There was me and then one more. He had the Down's Syndrome though, you know, and he only lived to be about ten for some reason. Nowadays that doesn't stop them at all. They grow up as good as anybody." One of her arms flailed out to the side and fell back down against her side in an exaggerated shrug.

The fat woman was embarrassed by this theatrical gesture. Trying to remember his name, knowing she should know the red-haired brother's name, she wondered what the pastor would think of the dramatic, flailing arm of her friend. She looked around quickly, willing to grant necessary apologies to onlookers who might have been offended. No one cared.

The red-haired woman was confused by the fat woman's overt glances. A funeral parlor is not the place to pass judgment on people's fashion sense. "But Dad never laid a hand on him, now."

"Oh. Of course not. It's unimaginable." They both ignored the shaky insecurity in her assertion that such things were.

The two women took an impatient step forward as the line inched along. They craned their necks to see who was paying last respects and to find out what could possibly be taking so long. A mother had picked up her little girl to let her look at the coffin. The little girl reached for the edge of the lid and pulled on it. The mother slapped her hand and put the little girl down. The little girl ran back down the aisle pushing through all the legs of people waiting in the receiving line. Her brother appeared from nowhere and followed her through the crowd. His hair was neatly combed and wet. He said, "Excuse me," to the red-haired woman. He moved quickly, careful not to run, and fidgeted with his tie. As the red-haired woman smiled down at him, the fat woman echoed with her own appropriate smile.

The red-haired woman revived their other conversation. "Why? Did your boys?" There was interest in her voice.

"Well, I would like to think not. But sometimes I suspected it. There was this one time with my middle boy, and he was just being secretive as you wouldn't believe. It made us both, me and Frank, just so uncomfortable.

Sometimes he would have the bleary eyes, you know. Broke my heart."

"I saw that on the news program once. About the eyes. With marijuana." The red-haired woman didn't say anything about buying a dime bag two weeks ago.

"Well, there was some strange cars come out to our place a few times, too. I told Frank we should ask him about it, but he thought we shouldn't get involved."

"But if he was in trouble why wouldn't you?"

The little girl ran back into the room slapping her patent leather shoes deliberately on the carpet. She ran past the flowers along the left wall until she came to a group of men in black and blue suits. She found her father and jumped up into his arms. Her brother stopped short, abandoning pursuit. The little girl rubbed her eyes to stop crying and wriggled up to the top of her father's shoulder. Defiantly, she stuck out her little pink tongue at her brother as the father patted her ruffled rear end. The brother receded.

"Well, Frank seemed to think it was just a phase and that he should work it out himself. And he did."

The little girl wriggled out of her father's arms. He set her down without notice and continued his conversation. The little girl ran off to find her brother on

the other side of the room. When she did, she pushed him
hard from behind.

"He's down in college now. He's studying some
kind of business. Seems to like it enough and doing real
good, too. He got a D in economics, but he never was as
good as his brother in math, so that figures. Otherwise his
grades are real good. He's not stupid, you know. Not at all.
Look at Marion. She looks frozen almost, doesn't she?"

"She was looking forward to seeing that boy's
college years. She never got to go."

"How could a child do that to his mother? I
couldn't go on living if one of my boys, or even Frank,
passed on."

"Frank's not going anywhere."

"No. I guess not."

The women were facing each other in the line,
talking more quietly now about the specifics. It wasn't
right, and they knew it. The red-haired woman was facing
the coffin with her arms crossed across her chest again.
The fat woman looked over the red-haired woman's
shoulder with an eye on the back door.

"A shotgun? Really? I didn't know that. I thought
his brother lived in Utah somewhere."

"He does. Wyoming. But he left his gun at home.
His grandfather gave it to him when he turned sixteen. He

wanted it to stay nice. It's an antique. Frank was real impressed when I told him what it was, but I forget now."

"That's one thing that I made Jim listen to. I said, 'No guns in the house.' You can see what can happen."

The fat woman saw a group of tall teenage boys come through the door together. She watched them all sign the guest book and mill around together. Presumably, they were five of the six starters from the high school basketball team. She recognized one of them as the younger brother of one of her son's friends. They looked so defeated. She couldn't watch. Young men are not supposed to be defeated. She moved herself around in line with the red-haired woman, and they faced the coffin side by side. There were still several people in front of them to greet the mother and pay their respects at the coffin. The fat woman was nervous. "Well, he did it out in the back barn."

"He was probably afraid Marion would crucify him herself if he got blood on that precious white carpet of hers."

"Oh, you are awful." Their conversation gained momentum. Together, with little words, they kept death at bay. It was hard work. They gave it their full attention, unconsciously.

"You'd never laugh as hard if you'd seen Michael when Marion told him to take off his shoes when we went over there to play bridge last fall. I laughed out loud. I have never seen that man without shoes in all the years we've been married. And here's Marion with that little flippant hair of hers telling my husband to take off his shoes.:

"Did he?"

"Of course! He had to. But we stopped playing bridge after that, except on holidays with my mom and dad."

"Oh, Lord. That is funny. With some of Frank's socks I would be embarrassed to have him take his shoes off." The people in front of the woman moved forward. They did not. The people behind them moved in closer. The women inched forward with the tiniest high-heeled steps.

"Oh, I know it. Especially walking on that white carpet she's got. It is pretty."

"Well, white carpet or not I would still rather have my son alive. Did you hear anything about why he did it?"

"Just bits and pieces. One of the kids had a friend who actually read the note he left."

"I didn't hear there was a note."

"Well, there was, and apparently it was about how he couldn't stand to watch his dreams become his friend's realities or something like that. All those years of dreaming big to watch other kids be able to pick up that stuff like it was nothing."

"Strange. How tall was he anyway?"

"Oh, I don't know; something like six-four. I'm not really sure. Michael would know."

"That basketball scholarship was only for tuition, and at a school that size, the cost of the dorm room and the books is more than twice what my youngest son pays for community college up north."

The fat woman had remembered the five boys. She glanced back at them in the line without really turning her head. Two of them were laughing and pushing against each other. The other three stood in a triangle with their feet and shoulders in line. All three left their hands forgotten behind them. They waited patiently as if the national anthem were about to start. Her eyes filled with fat tears and she replied with a shaky voice, "Oh. How is he doing? Community college, you say?" She cleared her throat and coughed into a torn-up tissue.

"Pretty good. He has that girlfriend of his, still, and they are living together now. Michael is not at all pleased, but she's on the Pill so she shouldn't be getting pregnant anytime soon. So I just keep my mouth shut and pray as much as I can." She wanted a cigarette.

"Oh. Well, bless your heart. I know I have been praying for Marion ever since I heard about this. So he wasn't going to take the scholarship then?"

"No. He would have had to work for his father, contracting."

"That's not so bad. Both my oldest boys did that for a few summers and made quite a bit of money." She was crying now.

The red-haired woman opened her purse and dug through it for a Kleenex. She did not look at the fat woman. "You know how they are at that age. Nothing is good enough. And plus remember that it wasn't just for a summer. This would have been a more permanent situation. He was just too proud for his own good." She pulled a wrinkled tissue out of a plastic package and handed it to the fat woman. "You should take what you are given and be thankful, if you ask me. I did, and I have been."

"I suppose. Still—"

"Oh well, I agree. It certainly is not cause to shoot yourself in the roof of the mouth." Too loud; way too loud. The people around them in line shifted uncomfortably. "He worked so hard to get away. His family still didn't have the money."

"His father must be devastated." She endeavored to push her eyeliner back in place.

"Well, sure. My God, that boy was his life. There was just the two boys, you know, and with the one off in Wyoming. I think they have other children, but just the two boys. That construction business has been going downhill ever since he started it, and I am sure this thing isn't going to do much for it."

"Maybe people will feel sorry for him and start coming."

"Well sure, at first, but then it will drop away to less than before." The arms were crossed over her chest again. The bra strap was almost to her elbow. Too many eyes were watching from behind her to fix it now. She really wanted a cigarette.

"I guess you're right. What kind of business is it, now?"

"He's a contractor. Builds farm buildings. Sheds, or whatever else."

The fat woman sensed irritation. "Oh. Right. Silly me. I still can't get over how long this receiving line is."

"We should have come an hour ago while people were still eating dinner." The skinny woman was irritated that the fat lady had been late.

Apologetically, "I just now got away. Frank's daughter from his first marriage has been visiting with her little girl."

"Has she? Now who is she married to?"

"Well, she's not. The guy ditched out on her. You know how they are."

"Of course I do. That's why Michael and I are so worried about our youngest living with this girl. Michael would absolutely die if one of our boys left a girl in a way. You know, that's how we got married."

"Really? I hadn't known that."

"Yes, I was two months pregnant before we even got married. No one knew."

"Of course not." Everyone had known, but it is important to protect yourself.

"But see, that's just it. Michael stayed, and he married me. And I know that's what he'd have his boys do." She would have added, "Damn fools that they are," but her eyes landed on the coffin and her words got tangled in a gasp.

"That was the old days, and Frank's poor daughter just got left. She's doing all right, and really, from what I have heard, this guy wasn't too good for her anyway. Still, it's someone to watch the kid for an hour so you can get away. Now I wasn't pregnant when I got married, but I was still pretty young. Frank was so much older, and he'd already been married. My parents just had a fit." The fat woman was licking the tissue and trying to fix her eye makeup. She noticed the red-haired woman wasn't really listening to her. "Well, anyway."

"We're getting closer."

"Yes."

"Marion looks nice, doesn't she?"

"She's a god damned angel."

"That's a bit extreme. All you see is the contrast. Without it, she's nothing special. Just one of us. Look. It's that dark hair she's got against her pale skin. It looks nice with the dark dress. She does have cute hair. I can never tell if it's brown or red."

"It's lovely."

"I couldn't wear my hair short. I would look like a chipmunk. I'd rather keep it long and put it up every day like I do."

"She can get away with it because she's got a slender face."

"She does."

"Marion."

"Thank you so much for coming."

"The flowers are gorgeous."

"I have never seen so many flowers."

"Most of my family is out west. They couldn't make it. Weather and holiday traffic at the airports. So the flowers are from them mostly."

The red-haired woman wondered how many families from out west travel extensively on Valentine's Day. "They're gorgeous."

Marion looked stunned. "Did you sign the guest book?"

The fat woman said, "I sure did."

"I will as I leave."

"Good."

"They are beautiful."

"So colorful."

"Yes."

The fat woman said, "Marion, we've both been praying so much. You will never be forgotten."

And the red-haired woman, the one who lived over on Fourth Street after she left her husband, after the night she broke out his back window when she found out how much he'd lost at the OTB by the interstate, agreed, "Oh yes, I haven't stopped praying since I heard."

"Well, thank you both so much. You know it really does help. It's so hard, but the thoughts are special and help so much."

"The wood is very pretty. Is that cherry?"

"I am not sure. It's the one he had here that we liked best. The others seemed suited to old folks more, you know."

"Well, good reason. You don't usually have teenagers dying at your house."

The three women stood stock-still pretending no shotgun had gone off, pretending no high school kid's mouth wrapped around any double-barreled shotgun, pretending no toe of his boot finally pressed the trigger back far enough, pretending that the back of his skull hadn't gotten blown across the barn, pretending no fathers ever found any sons dead.

It was the redheaded woman's responsibility to stop them all from thinking anything. She knew it. "It's nice that it's a closed casket."

Marion nodded. "They said it had to be. After we identified him, that was enough."

"Oh."

"Well. We will pray for you, Marion."

"Thanks for coming. It means so much."

The women fled down the aisle the same way the little girl and her brother had. Safe in the back of the parlor, they leaned in. The fat woman fumbled into her coat and the red-haired woman located her cigarettes and lighter in her purse.

"Oh shit, I can't believe I said that."

The fat woman tied a scarf under her chin. "I know. It was pretty bad, but don't worry about it. She is totally in shock."

"Dear soul." The lighter didn't work. She chucked it back into the purse and hoped for a forgotten book of matches at the bottom.

"Just sign the guest book. Let's get out of here."

"Sign for me. I need a cigarette."

"I signed when we came in and had no idea what to say. Plus, the pen wouldn't hardly work. Just leave it." Out of what was meant to be taken for a high-end crystal ashtray the fat woman picked up a gold book of matches with the name of the funeral home stamped on it in black and handed it to the red-haired woman. "All right then. It's been so good to see you. Sorry it's been so long. I know you called."

"Don't worry about it. We had a nice little chat right here tonight, huh?" She grabbed the matches and lit her cigarette on the threshold.

The fat woman held the door for her. "Sure."

"Say hello to Frank for me, would you?" The red-haired woman took a few thankful drags and looked up at the gray sky. She stamped her heels on the sidewalk to warm up a little. The red pickup was waiting at the curb. The fat woman was already making her way toward it.

"Of course. Same to Jim."

"Jim and I broke up twenty-five years ago. You know that. It's Michael now. But. Will do."

"I knew that. Sorry."

"It's not like we've been out much. Don't apologize."

"Why not? It's the only thing I'm good at." The fat woman laughed and opened the door of the truck carefully and climbed in. The truck leaned toward the curb. She closed the door quickly before it got stuck. She cracked the window of the truck and said to the woman on the sidewalk with a smile, "And keep those socks clean."

The red-haired woman waved back. She tried to think of something to say. She could not. The tears came instead. No real reason. They had good lives. Worthwhile lives. She wanted to yell at that stupid kid, and then she wanted to join him. Such a shitty small little nothing nowhere town. No one would miss her, really. Her kids didn't give a shit. Couple of pains in the ass after all she'd been through for them. But. No. Muster that smile for your friend. Don't flinch when you see her husband's arm reach out behind her back. Don't stop breathing when the pickup truck eases off on its way with the fat lady grinning and waving out the window. Don't get bitter. Just let the cigarette fall into the wet gutter from the height of a tall-as-you-can-ever-extend redheaded hand-wave.

PIETA

Solutions come easily when you cradle your dead son on your lap. More strict less strict understanding tolerant easygoing lots of hugs. There aren't any gray areas anymore. I know what I should have done for Jason, what I could have done for him. But it wasn't so easy when he came home drunk, so self-righteous, and so full of hard-edged life. I'd never admit it. Not even to my husband, Dan, but in my mind I called my son Genghis Khan. Because to have this massively disrespectful adult-sized child in my kitchen, with my collections of Longaberger baskets and antique swan figurines, was just beyond comprehension. I got so sick of his back talk. I wanted to beat the insolent belligerence out of him. Don't get me wrong; I never hit my child, but I did as much with words. Well not me, exactly. My husband was the enforcer.

I never questioned it. Because other people's children tiptoe in and try to sleep off their beers. Not my son. Seventeen, eighteen, nineteen, curfews didn't matter. He'd come into the house with an armload of empty beer bottles and dump them in my kitchen trash can. He never got sick; just wanted to eat. Invariably he'd cook something. Two in the morning and he'd have half the kitchen torn apart trying to make scrambled eggs or grilled cheese and bacon. Never anything simple like a bowl of cereal.

Upstairs I'd roll over and fret. My mind was in a constant tizzy about whether we should have done more of this or that. Everything that seemed like it might have been a mistake replayed to haunt me. Regret is not a strong enough word. I was dismantled. Night after night the world I tried to build came down. And it was never meant to be a dungeon for him, never a cell he was sentenced to as punishment. I wanted a fortress just to protect him, to keep him safe, to give him a chance. Because I knew no one would understand. People wouldn't love him like I did if they knew the truth. Maybe we'd been keeping secrets from him about some part of life he should have understood. But how could he know anything about what I did? He wasn't even born.

But that kid picked up on something. When he'd come home all clattering beer bottles like that, it's not that Dan and I weren't already awake waiting for him every time. We were usually in bed each pretending the other might be sound asleep. After twenty minutes of listening to dishes break and cans of corned beef hash fall on the tile, to the faucet running to overflowing and him banging around into everything, it was like a pattern. I'd say, "Maybe I should just go down and make him a real meal." Only after my suggestion did the man I married ever say, "No. No. You get some sleep, dear."

No one knew. Jason didn't look much different from his brother. But. Oh God. What I wouldn't do to have those three weeks of my life back. Dan forgave me, let me come home, and that was it. We moved on with our lives. Did everything we could for both our sons.

But Dan operated from this frightening sense of honor about the whole thing. So those nights when Jason came home drunk, when I was about to get up and go down to him, maybe even sit with him long enough to tell the whole story, my husband always did what he thought was the right thing. Dealt with it for me, you know? So he'd pat me and go downstairs. Exactly the same way every time. "No. No. You get some sleep, dear." And then two taps like I might have been a Labrador.

And that was it. Dan kicked off the covers, muttered, swore a bit to me, and went downstairs. He always started in on him the same way. "Damn it, Jason. Your mother is trying to sleep. What the hell do you think you're doing actin' a fool in my house? Are you drunk?"

Now even if me and my husband had a routine upstairs Jason had two different responses. He'd either laugh hysterically and go right on bumpin' into things, or he'd fly into an uncontrollable rage. Personally, I liked the rage better. They got everything out in the open. Sure they fought like hell. I half-thought they'd like to kill each other some of those nights. But they got exhausted quick and stormed off to bed within the hour.

If Jason laughed right in his father's face, though, those nights took a lot longer. Instead of screaming fits I heard taunting, jeering, and lectures. I never went down, but I could just see my Dan standing in the middle of our kitchen with his hands on his hips and his spindly little-old-man legs running down into those disreputable slippers, seething mad at the insolence, professing his infinite knowledge to the drunk cook. All the while I could hear Jason disrespecting his father, darting all around in the cabinets and the pantry looking for different things to throw into his late-night snack. Once they went on that way for more than three hours.

In the morning I'd clean up an incredible mess. There'd be the skillet with eggs, tomatoes, cheese, even chocolate chips cooked up and stuck to my Teflon.

Sometimes, instead of saying anything to my husband in our bedroom, I'd try to get to my son first. I'd get up and make a motion to go down before Dan so I could talk to Jason alone, make a little peace, maybe sedate him some. But I never made it farther than the landing. I guess it was a father-son time. Really those nights were about the only time those two were ever in the same room together. Jason avoided his father. Dan just seemed oblivious to his older son a lot of the time. He gets along better with Daniel. I try not to notice. Dan tries not to have it be true.

I wish I wouldn't have been so apprehensive those nights. I could have marched down the stairs like Cleopatra and told them both to go straight to hell or at least suggest they see some kind of psychologist. I knew there was something wrong, but I didn't know how to help. Guess it was the guilt, the shame. And just not believing that three weeks in a life matters much at all. If it would have been anyone else's kid, I would have had all the answers. You can see it better. Know what might help. But I acted like an idiot with my own son. I flashed him sappy smiles or reached out to touch him as he jerked

away. I don't know. I used to think he favored me. But I
don't know now. Maybe in some ways he didn't respect
me as much as he did his father. That's probably why I
never told him. He would have hated me, judged me,
judged himself.

But he should have known his story. And there
were times, dark times, lonely times, boring times in my
life when just looking at my son gave me so much joy.
Because he was a reminder of those three amazing weeks.
He had the same shape head as his real father. And
sometimes when I'd sit in my chair next to Dan, watching
the news or a movie in the evening with the kids, I'd just
look at the shape of Jason's head and be transported to a
place that made me smile. I couldn't live without Dan. But
that child was a true blessing to me his whole life.

Still. I don't know if he respected anything. I guess
he liked that job delivering milk and ice cream. He knew
every one of the restaurant, convenience store, and gas
station owners and managers in a forty-mile radius. Liked
his boss. Liked training the new guys. Ran two routes a
day when someone was out sick or if one of the guys'
wives was having a baby.

I fell into a habit of doing things for him that I
remembered he liked when he was little. Stupid, I know. I
baked cookies and left him little notes on the kitchen table

like I used to. I hope it comforted him a bit. He was having such a rough time in those years. With cancer patients—my mother died of cancer—at least you can dope them up on painkillers. You know they're suffering and there's something you can do for them. But there is so little you can do for someone like my Jason. It was just as chronic. I remember thinking that I was glad he drank because maybe it would numb some of that pain in his little lover-shaped head. I never said that to Dan. It's absurd to even think drinking's the answer. Most people would call me crazy. I think I was right, though.

But then I was just holding him there in the street. I knew I should have told him everything, should have defended my son to Dan, to the world.

I never could.

I remember how I heard the screech and how the transformer popped right before the electricity went out. Dan was on a business trip. I ran through the garden in my robe. I remember it felt like I was wearing a bedsheet. The cotton was too crisp and wouldn't move fast enough.

The car was smashed in on the passenger's side and the pole he hit had fallen. Electric lines hung slack and one was broken. Its two limp sinister ends swung slowly. I couldn't find him at first. Had to be careful of those live wires. I looked in the car, but he wasn't there. Usually

Victoria's security light floods three acres. But Jason hit whatever pole controlled that. I knew she'd make a call so I just kept running, looking everywhere.

There was a moon. It was that slack moon that always makes me uneasy, wishing for the beauty of phases that are more or less full. But thank God for the light of that slumped thing in the sky or I never would have found him.

He was thrown across the road. Almost into a ditch on the other side. He was so blue-white in that light. It made him look dead the minute I saw him. It was odd. You imagine a body just lying nice and flat, but he was all crumpled up. His right arm stuck straight out, falling down the slope of the new spring grass. His left arm must have broken because it just sank where something should have been bone. His left foot was on the road, but his right foot was way up under his chest.

His beautiful face got crushed half-slack just like that sorry moon. His head was twisted, his neck obviously broken, his mouth open with the top row of teeth sunk into the gravel and mud on the shoulder of the road. His tongue was hanging down in it. God. I sat there with his head in my lap for maybe fifteen minutes. Probably shorter than that, really. It was pitch black except for the moon and the stars.

Those so-called sweet birdies chuck their young out of the nest and if they can't fly—oh well. Can those parents possibly know? Do they have an instinct about when their chick is ready to fly? We didn't. Not really. We just figured by the time he was as old as he was he should be able to hack it.

Oh I knew everything for a moment. Everything about teaching responsibility and self-respect and obligation and fear. Sitting in that gravel, trying to lift his whole weight onto my lap, unable, and then with his crushed skull in my hands, like I could fix it, maybe, but no, as soon as he wasn't so vividly alive, I had answers. I gave myself pompous advice, came up with solutions about what to do with truth and lies. Dan goes to church a lot now I've noticed, but it doesn't help me much.

TANDEM

Going back in time and forward too, they drove across the western edge of the Eastern Time Zone and lost an hour. A carol recording played too loudly into the landscape at a Christmas tree farm in 2006. It was almost dark. The scent of hot spiced cider and gingerbread cookies came down from the barn where two matronly Midwesterners sat on folding chairs selling wreaths and centerpieces.

In the parking lot the Watsons' dog Squally ran ahead into the rows of evergreen trees, rummaging with her snout, discovering everything she could about the farm's firs and pines as the temperature continued to drop. A frozen crust of what hadn't melted during the warm part of the week covered rutted rows. Dan stopped at the edge of the lane and leaned against a post. "Damn." One boot sole was separating from the leather.

Marie moved on with her head bent down into the wind, following Squally's caprices. She had told him not to wear the boots. She stopped again and folded her arms across her chest. Her red turtleneck sweater and down vest weren't quite warm enough. She should have worn another layer. "Come on, honey." And she really wished she had a hat.

"But the boots. What about Dad's boots?" Catching up to her, whistling sharply for Squally to come back and stay closer, Dan fished through the pockets of his canvas coat and found an old black stocking hat. He handed it to his wife. "They're falling apart."

She did not think to thank him for the hat but held a bright-colored nylon leash, dingy from a year of use, in her hand and decided not to use it. She watched Squally bound off into the trees with pricked ears.

"Why aren't you saying anything? Didn't you hear me?"

Dan held a handsaw at arm's length and swung it in wide arcs almost like the pendulum dips of an amusement park's Viking ship ride which swings back and forth, up and down, hesitating at the heights before plunging down, releasing joyous screams of terror.

Marie looked at her husband who was walking awkwardly, trying to prevent more mud from getting inside his sock. "Those boots are probably forty years old! You're surprised they're falling apart?" She pulled the hat over the tops of her ears and looked at her own boots. Three hundred muddy dollars.

They got away from the tinny carol.

It was the eighth year of their marriage. Five years before Dan might have said, "Why didn't you put Squally on the leash? They don't want our dog running wild out here." But he just kept walking between the trees, swinging the handsaw and whistling *fweeeet!* when Squally got too far away.

The smell of gingerbread was gone.

Dan could not resist. "The kids should be here."

"They're too little and they're both sick, Dan. Why make sick kids ride three hours in the car, cold, dirty, and wet?"

"Don't you believe in tradition?"

She shook her head. "It was a tradition for your family, Dan. Not mine."

Christmas trees ran in different-sized rows in all directions.

He whistled for Squally again and grabbed the leash out of Marie's gloved hand. He knew what she was probably thinking—that an artificial tree like her mom's would be fine. But her mother's tree looked like a department store display. It was an eyesore of enormous bows, doves, angels. "Shake that self-righteous head all you want, Marie. But there will be no fake trees in my house. Ever."

She watched him clip Squally's collar and wrap most of the length around his hand. "Fine. But who was seven months pregnant last Christmas on the floor with the watering can getting needles in my eyes trying to keep that twelve-foot monstrosity alive, Dan? That thing drank a gallon of water a day. It filled two vacuum bags with needles in the first week. And was it you under that tree trying to keep it alive for six weeks? No, it was not."

"You always exaggerate." Dan kept Squally close, swung the old oiled saw absentmindedly from his other hand, and walked into one of the rows of blue spruce. "That was not a twelve-foot tree. We don't even have twelve-foot ceilings."

Marie waited in the lane until Dan was a good twenty feet ahead. She watched the distance increasing between them.

Squally barked, calling Marie forward into the row. It was that familiar friendly yip, the same sweet, clipped bark Squally used to announce that the baby's bottle had fallen out of the stroller, clattery plastic on concrete, rolling down the sidewalk. Still irritated with her husband, Marie picked her steps carefully in his footprints, keeping her boots as clean as possible.

They moved silently between the trees.

Marie could stop, scream, demand the keys, cry, insist on leaving, go sit in the car, take the dog off the leash again. But she didn't. She caught up to him. "Well, it was nine feet anyway. A nine-foot freaking monstrosity that put me into debt just to decorate." She pulled Squally's leash back into her possession.

The dog meandered along the full demonstrable generosity of leash length.

Dan's left foot was soaked inside the boot. He lifted his toes to protect them from the worst. This compensation added complexity to his gait. "Well, nobody died and made you Martha Stewart, Marie. You could have just spread out the decorations we had instead of drenching every single branch and then filling up the whole storage space with that overpriced tacky-ass shit."

"It's not tacky. It's Radko." She kept following Dan, giving Squally a tug. "Isn't there a Christmas tree farm closer to Chicago, Dan? Driving three hours is ridiculous."

"Every tree my whole life has come from this farm. I don't care if I have to drive ten hours; every year, every tree, as long as I can manage it, will come from this tree farm."

"And I'm self-righteous?" She tried not to think permanently-disabling thoughts about her husband. Why did they go through this every year? For what? For a Christmas tree? It was fine before the kids were born, kind of quaint, but now? They worked overtime all week. They still had a ton of shopping to finish, mostly to keep from hearing some litany of dissatisfaction from his mother. The old boots? The traditional tree farm? He was unbearable when he got like this—a nostalgic romantic who just would not let things go.

Marie unclipped Squally and watched the dog's silky coat ripple as she ran full force after a cardinal. "All this back-to-your-roots stuff gets old. There is no reason for us to drive all the way down here every year when the trees they sell right by us come from a bunch of farms just like this one. Your hick-ass, Puritanical bullshit only goes so far, Dan."

Dan shouted toward the sunset. "Squally!"

The dog disappeared into the darkening evening.

Marie pulled off a glove and felt the nearest branches.

An old man in insulated coveralls walked up to them from an adjacent row. "Finding everything, folks?" He kept a straight face and noticed Marie touching the trees. He forgave her unconsciously.

She winced and did not look at him. "You have any that don't drop needles?" It was caustic but not quite rude.

He ignored the tone. "We sure do. Scotch pine will do pretty good that way. I salvaged a few during the blight. Care if we drive out to the rows? It's too far for me to walk anymore."

Dan nodded his interest in the man's suggestion and ostentatiously took his wife by the hand.

They followed the old man to his truck, which was parked at an angle on a nearby rise.

He turned to Dan. "My eyes aren't so great with the light this low. Mind if I ride and you drive? It's a four-on-the-floor." He was not asking. He had already walked around to the passenger side and was helping Marie up into the truck. He closed the passenger side door and settled himself against it.

"It's been a while since I drove a stick." Dan put the saw in the bed of the truck, lowered the tailgate, and whistled.

"This old beast has had more clutches than I've had chicken dinners. Don't worry about grinding the gears. She can take it."

Squally came running and jumped up into the bed of the truck, an old pro at a new trick. She settled down to drowse on a tarp between the spare tire and the saw. Dan got into the driver's seat.

The old man watched Marie struggling to get comfortable between the two men and with the gearshift rising out of the floor of the truck. He said, "Now, I'm sorry, I didn't catch your name."

"Marie."

Slowly, emphasizing every single word, the old man said, "Okay. Now, Marie. I realize that this may not be the way you are used to riding. But I will tell you that most hick-ass women are not as Puritanical as you might think."

Marie flushed. "Excuse me?"

"There's not a one of them that doesn't know how to ride in the middle of a pickup."

Marie was nervous but trusted the laugh lines rooted deep at the edge of the old man's eyes. "I don't understand."

The old man looked out to the horizon and gave his instructions casually to the window. Letting his words make fog on the glass, he said, "Well, and I mean this with the utmost respect, dear. But you have got to straddle that thing and lean up against your husband so he can get to that shifter."

Marie's head snapped. She looked at Dan with wide eyes.

Dan shrugged, mouthing the words, "I don't know. It's his truck."

Marie managed to convince her designer jeans and her yes-I've-had-two-babies legs to straddle the gearshift. She let her left thigh rest against Dan's. She kept her right thigh from ever touching the old man's coveralls.

"Good. Now, Dan—wasn't it Dan?—just ease her back off this little embankment and take us up this lane about two hundred yards."

Dan put his hand over Marie's, who tried to hold onto his fingers with her gloves. He squeezed and let go. In the bed of the truck, Squally stood up, turned around twice, and lay back down again, contented by the truck's motion.

The old man looked at Marie and said, "You got any kids, Marie?"

Of course she had kids. Who doesn't have kids? She pressed her thigh against Dan's, encouraging him to relax and stop grinding the gears. "Two. The oldest is twenty-seven months. And the baby was born at the end of February."

"Good thing you didn't bring them. They'd catch their death out here today at those ages."

Marie leaped to the defensive. "Well, it was a tradition in Dan's family. So we would have brought them if we lived any closer."

"Bring them in a few years after they know all about Santie Claus. Then they'll never forget it." The old man nodded, agreeing with himself. "Go ahead and put it in third, Dan. Nothing to worry about out here. If you hit a deer, you won't even feel it. Truck's high-gauge steel. A regular tank. Drive as fast as you want. Hell. Open her up. We'll come back for the tree. Take us up to my property line at that strip of oaks."

Dan pressed his forearm against Marie's thigh while dropping the truck down into third and then fourth.

They passed well-maintained signage: Norway Spruce, Serbian Spruce, Concolor Fir, West Coast Noble Fir. The old man wasn't looking at the signs that marked the rows. He scrutinized the fence line as they bumped past it. Then all three—and Squally probably, too—watched the rushing fence posts. Keeping a keen eye out for any having fallen.

The old man turned back to Marie. "What tradition?"

Marie looked to Dan for approval to tell his story. Dan nodded, paying attention to the drive, loving the speed, loving the sound of frozen grasses shattering under the chassis.

"Dan used to come here, to your farm, every year when he was little. With his dad."

"Wasn't my farm then. I got this place five years ago in a foreclosure settlement."

Dan looked over. "Foreclosure? I thought you worked for the Loftons."

"Nope. At the worst of the blight this place just about got bulldozed for a housing development. Instead the Loftons held on as long as they could. Let the developers fish someone else's place over on 114. By the time they'd fought that fight they were so overextended that they couldn't make the property taxes. I got the place real cheap from the bank."

"But you always farmed around here?"

"No, ma'am. Not me. I was in real estate in Dayton for thirty-four years. I was married right after I got back from Korea. We had three kids: one smart one who can't keep a job for all his politics; one dumb one who can't keep her mouth shut but to say yes to any man dumber than her who comes along; and one who drives an old school bus from one art fair to another every summer and somehow manages to make a living painting hearts, flowers, and smiley faces on tiny wooden beads. Could have been a god-damned surgeon with steady hands like that—but nope, has to paint blessed beads."

Marie looked back into the bed of the truck to check on Squally. The happy mutt gave a cinnamon wag while watching the fence posts zip by under the dark blue broken clouds.

"Don't ask me why I did any of it." The man in coveralls rubbed the inside of the windshield with his sleeve and turned on the defrost blowers. "After I retired I had a charter-fishing boat business in Florida.

"But even in a subdivided paradise my wife hated me and made my life a living hell for as long as she walked this earth. No American dream for me, Marie. Not for me. Even though I edged my sidewalks clean and pretty in three damn states."

The oak trees held onto dry brown leaves. They all stared into the darkening woods. Dan downshifted and the truck stopped at the property line.

The old man cracked the window again. "I guess I could have divorced her somewhere along the line. Or

she could have divorced me. Or something. But that's
not what we did. We stuck it out. Did the best we could."

Marie said, "Sounds like you did great."

The old man laughed. "Some old milk slogan used
to say, 'Good as any, better than some.' That was us.
Good as any, better than some."

Marie was worried. "So you're all alone now?
You're way out here by yourself?"

"No, no, no, sweetie. I moved up here with my
girlfriend. Buying this place was her idea."

Dan sort of snorted. "Girlfriend?"

"Sure. In Florida, after my wife died, I'd get real
bored. Go down to the marina and tinker around on that
damned charter boat and end up at that little bar they had
there. Me and the other geezers all afternoon. Talking
about mangled manatees. What to do about oil leaking
into the channel. Whether to charge fathers for little
puking kids losing rods overboard—shit like that."

Marie reminded him. "But what about this
girlfriend?"

"Elaine? She never lost a rod. She wears a fishing
belt. She's no fool."

"I mean, how'd you meet her?"

"Oh, she ran a bait shop on the landing and sold
beer and candy and cigarettes, too. She ran the deliveries

to the bar in a motorboat. Somehow, I got to helping her unload that motorboat on her runs." The old man sat up straight.

The light was gone. The day was over.

After a long silence, the old man said, "Guess I didn't know about me hating my wife and my wife hating me while she was alive. Guess I thought all that antagonism, all that animosity, all that manipulation and the rest was love. How could I have known different? All those years should've meant something, right?"

"You didn't love your wife?" Marie folded her hands in her lap smoothing the finger of the glove over her wedding ring.

"Not like I love Elaine. Not like that."

The tradition was to implement a pattern that was a kind of suffering self-loathing to which any good person gets humbly indoctrinated. The tradition was to keep doing what you had always known how to do, to give up certain hopes for the someone whose role model said to love you. So what if you'd sacrificed almost everything on a little cross around your neck pulled side to side for years on end?

Marie turned to the old man. "What would you have done different?" She wasn't really asking to know.

"Nothing."

Dan said, "Nothing?" Dan looked back to be sure Squally was still there and not too cold. The dog was asleep.

The old man countered, "Good as any, better than some." He realized how late it was getting. "It's pretty dark to be picking Christmas trees now." But the old man wasn't sentimental. He wasn't a traditionalist. To him it was neither here nor there. He was a businessman. He motioned toward the darkness. "Well, you saw this place. Rows upon rows upon rows. And they're all the same anyway. Hell, we even spend the whole spring pruning so they're every one the damned same, exactly the same. I'll give you one of the precut Scotch pines half-price. No needles in the carpet this year, Marie. There's a six-foot beauty up there if Elaine hasn't sold it. It's plenty fresh."

Marie nodded, holding back tears. The tradition, Dan's tradition which kept the old man's heat on, was to walk into the unknown if familiar rows and pick your own tree, cut it down, carry it out any way you knew how, and call it yours until it died, until it was time, until it was time to let it go.

Throughout the evening the symmetric snowdrifts against the barbed wire fence changed from white to pink to lavender to purple-shadowed hillocks to blue to black and then back to white in the headlight beams.

The truck started up and Dan finally remembered how to drive in the country. He handled the old tank with surety. Marie watched him shifting gears between her legs. Squally must have woken up as they bounced and lurched over the frozen ruts.

LIMBIC RESONANCE: RESPONSES TO A MATCH.COM QUESTIONNAIRE

I

Me? You know how some women have those really nice sitting rooms? With the Ethan Allen furniture and the Andersen windows that open in, so that theoretically you can clean them easily on a regular basis? You know how you can hear that Windex squeaking in blue alcoholic circles which dissipate, right? You know how some women vacuum their stairs? Those soft almond stairs, with stripes like lawns, right? Well, I'm not really like that. I've got a plywood sitting room, with no furniture, where long-lost friends come and do gymnastics. I've got mirrors

which finally breathe light after years' dark storage box.
I've got shine and mercury filling up this column-spine.

II

Who I'd like to meet? Dear Lord, no more immovable
glaciers and, please God, no more rocky white waters,
jagged, choked, and swirling. Any other emotional
undercurrent? I can handle it. So hit me with your best
shot. Part of me wants to overcome this addicted-to-the-
thrill-ride part of my intimate life. I've read the self-help
books. I know it's pathologic and divisive. But it's not like
it's my problem. We're a generation of gimme sociopaths
playing dress-up and get-it-on. It's a cycle of heartbreak, a
norm of constant devolution, and I understand that it
breeds all sorts of instability that you can't call home. It's
consummate evidence of an insidious disrespect for
others. I have learned that nothing comes of it—that
people can get hurt, that nothing lasting exists in constant
resonance. I've learned a lot. But you know what? I'll tell
you what. I love believing in the aquifer. I love rivulets
trickling into silent secluded streams through limestone
beds. I love quick-moving rivers plunge-dive-bombing on
a sunny day. I love the immensity of oceans. I love

sublimation, evaporation, condensation, and I-think-it's-gonna-rain-soon thunderstorms. And honey—lovesick tenderized, meat cleaver runaway, undoing body surfer boy—I love those mighty waves. So, whatever I've learned, I'll see you curling bored in the pipe.

III

Do I want what? Who knows? Maybe. (Pass the gun, Mr. Walken. Let's go one more round of Russian roulette in these booby-trapped, mud-obscured Vietnamese waters. I'm up for it. Are you?) I suppose the main problem is that I don't want my children to have me for a mother. This creates a secondary problem wherein the only real logical choice is becoming someone other than myself, in order to have children, so that I can be their mother, successfully. Somehow logic gets lost. There's no way out of this bamboo trap. Not having children does not solve the syllogism. It should. But it doesn't. *(Faith enters stage left dressed in some sort of transparency.)* That's the kind of logic that doesn't last but finds a pocket in you somewhere to burrow down into, as if safe. That's the kind of momentary panic where you find yourself breathing in and out, real slow, real even, staving off something quiet.

IV

How? Isn't that sort of rude? I don't understand why so many people insist on discussing such things. Are there waves in the aquifer? As if it's anyone's business. Why do you ask? It seems there must not be. Can't be any kind of motion at all down there—memories are like that. Probably blind color-blanched fishes corroborate with stalactites and the drips. Silent. Still. Refusing to thrash, to be heard. Probably something calcifies and the surfers get bored waiting for conditions to change. Well, if you must know: Introvertigo; Extrovertigo. I come and I go. How do you do it? On Wednesday mornings with the light pouring in through slatted blinds? Isn't that sort of trite? I do it. I do it fine with tree frogs starting to sing when the shower-timers go off in their cages at 4:00 a.m. in some old boyfriend's memorable trailer. Probably waves that do get started panic underground, sealing, and escape any way they can. Introvert, I go. Extrovert, I go.

V

Regardless: No, I'm not doing anything this weekend. What do you want to do?

ABOUT THE ON IMPULSE SERIES

The War is Language: 101 Short Works

2000 Deciduous Trees: Memories of a Zine

Love & Darts

Acquainted with Squalor

Radar Road: The Best of On Impulse

We each have an impulse to share our experience. These four collections of short works explore storytelling from catharsis to craft. Over the course of this series Nath Jones's writing style develops from the raw, associative, tyrannic rambles of cathartic non-fiction, flash fiction, and rant in *The War is Language* and our digital domains, to the delightful rough-hewn vignettes of *2000 Deciduous Trees*, into the compact characterizations of the fictionalized tellings in *Love & Darts*, and finally toward *Acquainted with Squalor's* fully-crafted short stories that use literary devices and narrative elements to reveal a world well-rendered.

ABOUT THE AUTHOR

Best New American Voices nominee Nath Jones received an MFA from Northwestern University. Her publishing credits include *PANK Magazine*, *There Are No Rules*, *The Battered Suitcase*, and *Sailing World*. Her current series, *On Impulse*, explores the spectrum of narrative from catharsis to craft. She lives and writes in Chicago.